'Coming on

Selina gasped. 'Y... just like the rest ... under the impress... ... one husband, I'm on the ... ...other…or the equivalent of.'

Her voice broke on a sob and he flinched.

'It's not like that,' she choked. 'I just want to be left alone.'

Kane bit into his bottom lip with even white teeth. If he'd wanted to break through Selina's reserve, what better way could he have found? But what a fool to make such a comment!

'I'm sorry, Selina. I spoke without thinking. It's just that in the past I have been propositioned and…well, I don't like it. So do please dry your eyes and tell me I'm forgiven for being such an insensitive clod.'

She threw him a watery smile.

'You're forgiven. I'm afraid I'm very touchy these days… And, Kane…?'

'What?'

'I'm not surprised you've had to fight them off.'

Abigail Gordon loves to write about the fascinating combination of medicine and romance from her home in a village in Cheshire, England. She is active in local affairs and is even called upon to write the script for the annual village pantomime! Her eldest son is a hospital manager and helps with all her medical research. As part of a close-knit family, she treasures having two of her sons living close by and the third one not too far away. This also gives her the added pleasure of being able to watch her delightful grandchildren growing up.

Recent titles by the same author:

EMERGENCY RESCUE
THE NURSE'S CHALLENGE

PARAMEDIC PARTNERS

BY
ABIGAIL GORDON

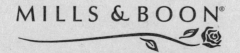

For Helen, and those who work with her

*All the characters in this book have no existence outside the imagination
of the author, and have no relation whatsoever to anyone bearing the
same name or names. They are not even distantly inspired by any
individual known or unknown to the author, and all the incidents are
pure invention.*

*First published in Great Britain 2002
Harlequin Mills & Boon Limited,
Eton House, 18-24 Paradise Road, Richmond, Surrey TW9 1SR*

© Abigail Gordon 2002

ISBN 0 263 83090 X

*Set in Times Roman 10½ on 11½ pt.
03-0902-51399*

*Printed and bound in Spain
by Litografía Rosés, S.A., Barcelona*

CHAPTER ONE

THE breakfast pots had been washed, the beds made, the washer switched on, the letter from her father-in-law in the morning post dutifully read, and now Selina was about to top up her tan on a sunlounger in the back garden.

Creamed against the powerful rays of a midsummer sun and wearing a black bikini, she was looking forward to some prime time by herself. Shutting her ears to the noises coming from the main street of the village, which was only yards away, she sank down thankfully onto the soft upholstery.

Two whole days, she thought thankfully. Time to recharge her batteries before going back on the unit for night duty.

Tomorrow there was to be a fête on the village green they might go to, and there was a film on in the town centre that she wouldn't mind seeing afterwards.

But today she was going to potter. Sunbathe for a while, have a leisurely lunch and then later make a nice meal for the two of them.

When the phone rang she groaned. Letting the magazine she'd brought out with her fall to the ground, Selina eased herself off the sunbed and padded inside.

The voice at the other end of the phone belonged to the head teacher at Josh's school, and her face blanched as he said in subdued tones, 'I'm glad I've caught you in, Mrs Sanderson. I'm afraid that your son has had an accident.'

'What do you mean?' she cried. 'What kind of an accident?'

'He ran out of the school yard onto the main road to

retrieve a ball during breaktime and into the path of an oncoming car.'

Don't let him be dead, she prayed as dread turned the blood in her veins to ice. Not my little one. I can't take any more.

'We're not sure how badly hurt he is,' he went on. 'We haven't moved him under the circumstances and an ambulance is on its way.'

So at least Josh was alive, she thought frantically, but for how long?

'Tell the paramedics to wait for me,' she shrieked into the receiver, and before he'd had time to reply she was flinging open the hall cupboard and throwing on a long raincoat to cover the bikini, at the same time forcing her feet into the nearest footwear to hand, which happened to be the trainers she wore for jogging.

She was at the junior school on the outskirts of the village within minutes, and she didn't have to search for the scene of the accident. The ambulance was already there, standing purposefully at the kerbside outside the gates. Even if it hadn't been, the crowd that had gathered would have been indication enough.

As she flung herself out of the car and began to push past the onlookers with frantic haste, Selina's horrified gaze was on the small figure of her son, lying very still at the pavement edge.

A paramedic was bending over him and another was stepping down from the ambulance with a red response bag in his hands.

'I'm his mother,' she cried, falling to her knees on the other side of the small casualty with hands outstretched to do the things she'd done countless times...for other people's children.

The man bending over her son was examining him with deft yet gentle hands. Beside herself with panic, she cried,

'Have you checked that he's breathing? For spinal injuries? That his tongue is free? That his tubes aren't—?'

He didn't lift his head.

'Yes. I have,' he informed her levelly, 'as far as is possible under the circumstances. Now we need to get the boy to hospital as quickly as possible.'

'Roll him onto a backboard,' she ordered. 'I don't want Josh risking further injury by being handled too much.'

Selina wasn't aware of the brief appraisal of a pair of dark eyes, or that the man's voice when he spoke again wasn't quite as impersonal as before.

'We're going to do that. So if you would, please, stand back?'

She could hardly bear to move an inch away from Josh, but heaven forbid that she should behave like other hysterical relatives she'd seen, hindering the progress of the ambulance team.

'I'm coming with you,' she cried.

'Of course,' he said crisply, and within seconds they were off, with the siren blaring and the light flashing above the fast-moving ambulance with its distinctive coloured flashes.

Instinctively Selina reached across for the advance support bag containing the equipment that would be needed if Josh went into cardiac arrest or if his airways became blocked. But a voice from beside her, which was heating up by the moment, cried, 'Do you mind? I'm in charge of this vehicle. You may be the boy's mother, but I'm the paramedic and I have everything under control. At least I would have if you could resist trying to take over. I understand your great anxiety but do, please, leave it to me.'

As if realising for the first time that he was in charge, Selina just sat and blinked at him.

'As you can see,' he continued, 'we have your son on a backboard to prevent further spinal injury, should there be any, and we've tied his legs together as the left one is almost certainly fractured. The cuts on his head and arms are mostly superficial, except for the gash on the temple…and I will be monitoring his heart all the time we're in transit. Does that satisfy you?'

The younger man, who had taken over the driving, turned his head at that moment. He could have been invisible for all the notice Selina had taken of him so far, but now he was registering, and when he spoke she recognised the voice and the face.

'She's one of us, Kane,' Mike Thompson explained.

In his second year of training, and referred to by those in the know as an ambulance technician, he was a reserved sort of young man who never had much to say, but it was obvious that he felt some sort of explanation was due, and towards that end he went on to explain awkwardly, 'Selina's on the unit.'

The other man groaned, and said to Selina, 'So that's why you're trying to take over. I get the picture.'

At that moment Josh opened his eyes, and as he did so both men were once more blurred figures on the edge of her nightmare.

'Mum, I hurt all over,' he said tearfully. 'I was hit by a car. Where's Dad?' He'll make it better.'

'I know what's happened, my darling,' she said softly. 'You're in an ambulance on the way to hospital. They'll make you better there.'

'I want my dad,' he wailed. 'It's not fair.'

Selina swallowed hard. In the shock of the accident Josh was trying to put the clock back and, aware of the man hovering watchfully beside her, she said soothingly, 'I know. But you do know that he would have been here if he could, don't you?'

Josh nodded glumly and turned his head into the flat pillow beneath it.

'So he can move his neck,' the strange paramedic said. 'That's good. And apart from the fractured limb, the rest of him seems to be flexible enough. They said at the school that the car driver wasn't going very fast and that your son bounced sideways off the bonnet, which probably saved his life.'

Selina nodded bleakly. It was something to be thankful for, but there would be questions she would be asking about supervision in the playground. Though at the moment all that mattered was Josh.

The ambulance was turning into the hospital car park and as she raised herself from her kneeling position beside her son, the old coat that she'd flung on swung open and an expanse of bare midriff was briefly on view.

She must look like nothing on earth, she thought raggedly as she clutched it to her. Trainers, the briefest of bikinis…and a raincoat that didn't button properly. A far cry from the neat navy trousers and crisp white blouse that would have been her normal attire had *she* been taking a call-out such as this while on duty.

As the bossy paramedic wheeled Josh into Casualty, Selina was beside him, holding his hand and hoping that Gavin would be on duty.

He was. He'd just come out of one of the cubicles, and as he swished the curtains together behind him he saw them.

His glance went first to Selina's white face and then flicked to Josh.

'What's happened?' he asked as he hurried across to them.

'Josh has been knocked down by a car,' she choked out. 'The paramedic says he has a fractured leg and there might be other injuries.'

Light blue eyes in a tired face met hers. 'And what's your opinion?'

'I'm so worked up I can't even think straight.'

He patted her shoulder briefly. 'Let's get him sorted then, shall we?'

The moment Josh was rolled off the backboard onto the bed in an empty cubicle, Mike Thompson and his unknown colleague stepped back, their job done, and at that point Selina began to calm down a little.

Now that Josh was in hospital, with Gavin there to take over and with a nurse hovering, she was able to take stock of the man who must obviously be Charlie's replacement.

Selina had worked with Charlie Vaughan ever since joining the ambulance unit, and now, at the end of her second year of training, she was having to part company with the man who had been with the ambulance service for thirty years and was about to retire.

If it hadn't been for Charlie's never-failing good humour and infinite patience during that time, both with herself and those he served, Selina knew she might have given up.

The hours were long, and there was always trauma of one kind or another awaiting them when a call came through, but there was job satisfaction, too…lots of it.

Charlie had said the other day that a paramedic from another area was to replace him and Selina had a feeling that the man eyeing her unsmilingly from the other side of Josh's bed could be he.

He was tall and loose-limbed, with a shock of dark hair above a face that might have been described as hawk-like if it hadn't been so arresting. His eyes were deep brown and very cool, his mouth a straight line, and she had a sudden sinking feeling that partnering this man was going to be a different ball game to working with Charlie.

'Kane's replacing Charlie,' the monosyllabic Mike said, as if reading her mind, and Selina nodded, while the man in question continued to eye her silently.

What was the matter with him? she thought irritably.

He'd had enough to say in the ambulance. Maybe he was waiting for some comment from her? Meeting his glance, she said stiffly, 'I see. I thought that might be it, but I'll have to ask you to excuse me. All I can think of at the moment is that my son is hurt.' Her voice broke.

'I took him to school myself,' she croaked to no one in particular. 'Saw him safely into the playground and watched his class file in and now…now I'm told that he's been knocked down by a car.'

'I'm sending Josh for X-rays on his leg and spine,' Gavin said gently. 'Buck up, Selina. He'll be frightened if he sees you upset.'

She blinked back the tears that were threatening.

'Yes, you're right. Let's go, then.'

The man in the white coat, who was as familiar to her as her own face, nodded. 'I'll be waiting when you get back,' he promised.

When she looked up, Mike and the new man had gone. Back to base, no doubt, to await the next red alert or whatever else came through that needed their attention.

As they set off down the corridor, with the nurse pushing the bed and Selina holding tightly onto Josh's hand, Gavin called after them. 'By the way, I like the outfit, Selina.'

She managed a smile.

'I was sunbathing.'

'I'd never have guessed,' he said with a smile of his own.

Josh had been lucky. The X-rays showed no spinal injuries, but he *had* sustained a fracture of the tibia of his right leg. The break was across the shaft, for which Selina was thankful as fractures of the lower part of the tibia often resulted in a fragmented ankle bone that had to be repaired by surgery, whereas in Josh's case, a plaster cast on the leg for approximately six weeks should see the bone healed.

'I'm keeping him in for a couple of days just as a precaution,' Gavin said when the cast had been applied, 'and as it goes without saying that you won't be budging from his side once he's settled into the children's ward, why not go home and change out of your fancy dress? I'll keep an eye on Josh until they find him a bed.'

'I might just do that,' she said. 'I'd hate your staff to think that your sister's eccentric…and, dear brother, am I glad that you've chosen to do a stint in Accident and Emergency.'

He shrugged. 'In a crazy sort of way I'm enjoying it. It's a case of you ambulance folks bringing 'em in, and my lot sorting 'em out.'

Selina shuddered. 'And in this case it was Josh that they wheeled in. I can't stop thinking that he might have been killed.'

As she was making her way to the main reception area to telephone for a taxi she saw the two paramedics coming towards her. Remembering how her introduction to the new man had been somewhat heated, Selina said awkwardly, 'I see you're back already.'

'Yes,' he said. 'Another red alert came through before we'd got back to base and, having delivered the patient to A and E once more, we're on our way back again. How's the boy?' he went on.

'He's got a fractured tibia, which has just been put in plaster, and my, er…Gavin is keeping Josh in for a couple of days. There were no obvious spinal injuries, but he isn't taking any chances and wants to keep him under observation for a while.'

He nodded.

'Good.'

Dark eyes were flicking over her and momentarily a smile tugged at his mouth.

'I take it that you're going home to change. We'll drop you off if you like.'

'I'm starving,' Mike put in. 'If you're taking Selina home, I'll have a bite in the restaurant here and you can pick me up on the way back.'

Selina hesitated. Another encounter with the man who was going to be featuring prominently in her working life in days to come didn't appeal. But for him to take her home and bring her back almost immediately when he came to pick up Mike would be so much quicker than any other way, and she didn't want to be away from Josh for a moment longer than necessary. He was happy enough with his Uncle Gavin, but it was her he needed the most...and his absent father.

But if she started thinking about Dave she would go to pieces completely and that wouldn't help anybody, especially Josh.

She smiled.

'That's an offer I can't refuse. I'm so anxious to get back to Josh.' She looked down at the shapeless raincoat and, thinking of what it was concealing, told him, 'I was sunbathing when I got the call from the school and I threw on the first things that came to hand. I don't remember if I locked the door even, so I do need to go home for a few minutes.'

'Let's get moving, then,' he said flatly, as if he thought she was gabbling somewhat.

When she climbed in beside him Selina was aware that, if what Mike had said was correct, this man was replacing Charlie. That was how it was going to be in future, and a bigger contrast to the amiable sixty year-old she couldn't imagine.

As they pulled out of the city limits he said, 'I suppose I'd better introduce myself.' Taking a hand off the steering-wheel for a moment, he offered it to her. 'Kane Kavener is the name, and the station officer has told me that you and I will be working together.'

His grasp was firm as they shook hands briefly. Selina thought illogically that it was like the man as there seemed to be nothing limp about...what was it he'd said his name was? Kane Kavener?

'What they've told you is correct,' she confirmed as their hands fell apart. 'Charlie Vaughan, who I've worked with ever since joining the ambulance service, retired yesterday and so I'm short of a partner.'

'So, what stage of training are you up to?' he asked. 'You're not a paramedic?'

Selina shook her head.

'No. Not yet. But I hope to be soon. I've done my year as a trainee and am almost at the end of a second year as an ambulance technician. As we both know, the next step is to take my paramedic exams.'

'Who looks after the boy while you're working?' he questioned. 'His father?'

'Er...no. My brother and his wife live nearby and she looks after Josh, along with her own two children, while I'm at work.'

He nodded.

'I see.'

Selina was observing him warily. What was he doing? Assessing her to see if she would be pulling her weight when they were on call-out? Or what?

'How old is Josh?'

'Nine,' she replied briefly, 'and he's an only child.'

She was beginning to feel as if it was time that she did a bit of probing of her own.

'Where have you moved from?' she asked casually.

'I've been living and working down south. This is my first experience of a northern city. I'd hoped to settle here a couple of weeks ago to give me some breathing space, but something cropped up and I only arrived yesterday.'

'And you're already on the job!' she exclaimed. 'That seems a bit much.'

He shrugged as if it was of no consequence. 'My contract said that I start today, and today it is.'

She was giving him directions and he said, 'I take it that *working* in the inner city is enough. You don't choose to live there?'

'That's correct. I live in a Pennine village that isn't too far away for commuting and is a better place to bring Josh up in.'

When they stopped outside the neat stone cottage, which had seemed like a paradise when Dave had been around and now was just a place to live, Kane settled back into the driving seat and said, 'I'll wait. Do whatever you have to do. If any calls come through, I'll radio back to base and explain what's happened and where I am.'

Selina hesitated. The least she could do was invite him in.

'Don't wait out here. You can make yourself a drink while I'm changing.'

'You're sure?'

'Yes.'

He opened the door and stepped onto the pavement, observing the house as he did so.

'Nice. Have you always lived in the area?'

She nodded, wishing as she did so that he would leave it at that.

He did and, after directing him into the kitchen and showing him where she kept tea, coffee and suchlike, she went into the hall and took off the drab raincoat.

Selina paused for the briefest of moments as the bikini was revealed. She sighed. It seemed like a lifetime since she'd padded out into the garden to sun herself.

Framed in the mirror opposite was a woman with straight golden hair fastened back in a ponytail, slender almost to the point of being too thin, with violet eyes behind long lashes and a kind mouth.

The men on the unit often joked that she should be on the catwalk instead of the paramedic treadmill, but she only laughed when they said it. Ever since she'd joined the St John's Ambulance Service while still at school Selina had known where she was heading.

But her mother's long illness, her father's incapacitation until he, too, had passed away and then becoming pregnant with Josh almost as soon as she and Dave had married had put a hold on career plans until a couple of years ago.

At that moment the kitchen door swung back and Kane Kavener was standing there with the coffee-jar in his hands.

'It's empty. Shall I er…?' His voice trailed away when he saw her, and there was something in his glance that made her face grow warm.

'Open a new one? Yes. You'll find one in the cupboard,' she said quickly, and with an about-turn she ran up the stairs.

Within seconds she was back down, dressed in a white cotton top and denim cropped trousers, and carrying a small holdall.

He put down the mug he was holding and with the other hand replaced the photograph of Dave and herself that he'd picked up from the window shelf.

'Your husband?' he asked casually.

'Yes,' she told him quietly, 'and if you're wondering why he isn't here when his son is asking for him…'

He raised his hand with palm outwards to halt the flow of words.

'Not my business. It just seemed a shame, that was all. Josh wanting him and him not being there, but fathers have a living to earn. They can't always be around.'

'Dave is dead,' she told him tonelessly. 'He died of cancer a year ago.'

Kane's face went slack. 'I'm sorry. So sorry! It must be very hard for you.'

'It is,' she said simply. 'But there has never been anyone to tell us that life is fair, has there?'

'No, indeed,' he agreed soberly.

Wishing that she'd been a bit less upfront with her affairs, she said, 'Are you ready?'

'Of course...and make sure that you lock up this time.'

Not another word passed between them on the way back but Selina thought that she'd said enough already, considering they'd only met hours ago. But at least he would have her sussed for when she turned in for duty—he would have found out her circumstances sooner or later.

Kane Kavener hadn't been very forthcoming about himself, though, had he? A quick glance at his inscrutable profile was a reminder that if she'd been upfront about herself to the man who was to be her new partner, he wasn't prepared to paint a picture of himself for her.

When he stopped on the hospital forecourt he spoke for the first time.

'I'm told that you're due back on duty the day after tomorrow, and that would have been our first day together, but obviously your son's accident will have changed that.'

Selina nodded.

'Yes. I'll be staying with Josh until he comes out of hospital and will want to be with him the first few days after he comes home while he adjusts to the plaster cast and moving around on crutches. Once that's sorted he'll be all right with my sister-in-law, Jill.' She cast an anxious glance at the door marked OUTPATIENTS. 'Just as long as there are no unforeseen complications from the accident.'

'I hope that won't be the case for both your sakes,' he said gravely, then added, with his voice lightening, 'Can I take it that you won't be bossing me about when we start working together?

She gave a weak smile.

'You mean like this morning?'

'Hmm. Although I do admit there were extenuating circumstances.'

'You'll have to wait and see, won't you?' she said smoothly, and on that note she opened the door and was gone.

Josh had just been settled into the children's ward when she got there, and now that his leg was more comfortable and his cuts and bruises had been treated he was feeling more cheerful and ready to enjoy the novelty of the situation he found himself in.

When Selina appeared at his bedside he looked up at her with the bright blue eyes that were so like Dave's and said, 'I know that Dad is dead, Mum. I don't know why I said what I did.'

'You were hurt and frightened, my darling,' she said softly, 'and wanted your dad as well as your mum. It was understandable, and although Dad isn't with us anymore he'll be watching over you somewhere, I'm sure.'

He was smiling.

'Do you think they have traffic accidents in heaven…like when they get onto the wrong cloud or have a skid on the Milky Way?'

Selina laughed and there was relief in it because he was joking about Dave now, not crying for him.

Gavin had gone off duty. By now he would be home and would have told Jill what had happened. Her sister-in-law, who was also her closest friend, would be horrified.

By nine o'clock that evening Josh was fast asleep after his distressing day, and one of the nurses on the children's ward said, 'He's happy enough with us, Mrs Sanderson. Why don't you go home and get some rest? We'll ring you if there are any problems.'

'All right,' she agreed reluctantly, 'but I'll be here by six o'clock in the morning.'

Gavin and Jill lived in a big Victorian semi by the village green and, before letting herself into the cottage, Selina called in to see them.

'How awful for you both!' her petite sister-in-law said, hugging her close. 'Whatever were the school thinking of to let Josh run out on to the road like that?'

'I don't know,' Selina said sombrely, 'but I have a feeling that it might have been his own fault. He tells me that when the ball went over the wall his friends were all urging him to go and get it and while the playground supervisor's back was turned he lifted the chain off the gate and ran out. But even so I shall be having a talk with the headmaster once I've calmed down.'

Gavin sighed. 'Show a boy a ball and he undergoes a complete change of personality. How is he now?'

'He was asleep when I left him, but I'll be back there first thing.'

In the double bed that she'd once shared with Dave, Selina found she couldn't sleep. Pictures of the day's happenings kept going through her mind like shots from a horror movie, and mingled with them was the memory of the meeting with her new partner, Kane Kavener.

Where was *he* sleeping tonight? she wondered. He would have finished the day shift at seven o'clock and what then? Gone for a meal? Finished his unpacking? Or was there someone waiting for him, eager to hear how his first day had gone?

Why had she been in such a hurry to tell him she was a widow? she asked herself. She hated the sound of the word. For one thing it was a reminder that Dave wasn't around any more, and for another it was like having a badge pinned on her, indicating that she was once again available. A marriageable woman. But not without strings attached. The 'string' in her case was an adorable fair-haired boy, whom she could have lost if a certain motorist hadn't been driving slowly...and hadn't clapped on his brakes as fast as he had.

Maybe at the back of her mind, when she'd said what she had, had been the memory of a couple of passes that men had made at her in recent weeks.

She'd quickly rebuffed them and afterwards had thought tearfully that she hated being in the position of a lone woman.

And so why should it be any different with him? she asked herself. She didn't know. But something about Kane had told her that he wasn't the chatting-up type. And why, for heaven's sake, was she taking it for granted that he might be even remotely interested in anything concerning her?

In the end she got up, showered, made herself a quick breakfast in the summer dawn, then set off for the hospital once more.

Josh was discharged on Sunday morning, and as he swung himself along the garden path on a small pair of crutches Selina was just glad to have him home again.

'One of the paramedics came in to see me last night after you'd gone, Mum,' he'd said earlier when she'd arrived on the ward.

'Really! Which one?'

'The new one...Kane.'

'That's strange!' she exclaimed. 'He would have been off duty by then.'

'Mmm, he was. He brought me some comics and sweets...and told me to look where I was going in future. He asked where you were and I said you'd gone home to have a rest.'

'I see.'

She didn't really. It had been a kind thought, but was it because he was sorry for them both?

Jill, Gavin and their three-year-old twin daughters called round in the afternoon, and after the tension of the last few days it was nice to have the house filled with noise and laughter.

'So what about next week?' Jill asked as they were leaving. 'When are you going back to work?'

'Not until I'm happy to leave Josh,' she told her. 'You've got your hands full with the twins and I don't want to make life difficult for you.'

'You won't be,' Jill told her serenely. 'We're used to having him around and the twins are fascinated by the crutches.'

'Then in that case I might go in on Tuesday. I should have been on nights today and tomorrow, but the station officer has arranged for one of the other trainees to fill in for me. Which means that I'll be going back to day shifts.' She paused and then added meaningfully, 'With my new partner.'

'And who might that be?' Gavin asked.

'The paramedic who came out to Josh.'

'So you've already met?'

'Yes, we've already met,' she said glumly.

He laughed.

'And what did he think of your trendy outfit?'

What had he thought? she wondered. Especially when he'd seen what had been under the raincoat.

'Cheer up, sis,' he said reassuringly. 'Wait till he sees you in action. You'll knock him cold.'

'I hope not,' she said with gloom still upon her. 'He's not exactly the warmest person I've ever met.'

CHAPTER TWO

AS HE'D let himself into a soulless flat in a high-rise block in the city centre on the Friday night, Kane's mind had been on his meeting with Selina Sanderson earlier in the day.

First there'd been the ride in the ambulance when, mother of the victim or not, he'd wanted to throttle her for trying to take over.

At that time he hadn't known who she was, and he'd been thinking ever since what a bizarre way it had been of getting to know each other.

Then there'd been the brief visit to her home and the glimpse of what she hadn't been wearing beneath the raincoat. She was quite something in an understated way, he thought as he filled the kettle at a well-used stainless-steel sink.

It was sad that she'd lost her husband so young. Even more sad had been the youngster crying for the dad he wasn't ever going to see again.

As he soaped himself under the shower it occurred to him that it was the first time in days he'd thought about anyone but himself.

It had taken the frantic young mother and the injured child to make him take a good look at himself, and he wasn't too chuffed at what he was seeing.

You need to snap out of it, he told himself. It's over and done with. You came out of it with your reputation untarnished, so what's the problem?

It didn't make him feel any less angry, though, and future working partners of the opposite sex would be kept at a wary arm's length...even if they were leggy, blonde and appealing.

He'd never had trouble with women before. They were attracted to him for some reason and he'd had some pretty interesting relationships.

Yet they'd never lasted. There'd never been anyone that he'd wanted to make a commitment to. Of all things, he didn't like to be pursued and that was how it had been with Eve Richards.

It still made his skin crawl when he thought about what she'd done, even though it had come to light that there'd been extenuating circumstances.

He'd decided to move as far away as he could get from her, and when she'd found out Eve had complained that she'd been sexually harassed by him.

If he hadn't been so devastated it might have been amusing, as *she* had been the one guilty of that. From the moment she'd been assigned to him as an ambulance technician she had been like an infatuated limpet. Touching him whenever the opportunity arose. Buying him gifts. Inviting him out to lunch. And in the end blatantly asking him to sleep with her.

If she'd been the last woman on earth he wouldn't have wanted to do that. She was reasonably attractive in a sloppy sort of way, but definitely not his type, and in the end he had asked for her to be partnered with another woman.

The station officer had been sympathetic, but new rotas and staff shortages had meant that the move had been a long time coming and in the end Kane had decided that the only thing to do had been to remove himself from her orbit.

There was a hysterical scene when she knew he was going and the next thing was the complaint against him. It was his word against hers and he knew with a sinking feeling that a woman was often believed in that sort of situation.

But where the station officer had been slow in the first instance, he moved quickly when the complaint was made and had the authorities delve into Eve Richards's records.

They discovered that she'd been treated for a severe mental disorder in the past and it had been overlooked when she'd applied to join the ambulance service.

It made him feel less angry with Eve but furious with those responsible for *him* having to endure such harassment, even more so because their patients could have been put at risk by her unstable behaviour.

For weeks he didn't know whether he was coming or going. Whether he would be suspended. Whether the position in the north that he'd accepted would be lost if he couldn't take it up on the date specified.

A date for a disciplinary hearing was set and it was very near to the time when he was due to move to Cheshire to start the new job. He was summoned to attend and did so, angry at the kind of limbo he found himself in.

However, the medical evidence regarding Eve's state of mind was so conclusive that before he knew it he was cleared of the charge.

The relief was exquisite, and though those in authority tried to persuade him to stay he was adamant that he was leaving.

And now here he was. In a dingy flat which was all he could find at such short notice.

He wondered if he would have been so aware of its shortcomings if he hadn't been to Selina's cottage in the delightful Pennine village. Maybe he ought to move in that direction when he started house-hunting…just as long as no one was going to get any wrong ideas.

With mother and child still on the edge of his consciousness, he popped in to see the boy on Saturday night when his shift was over.

It was done on impulse. He'd gone to buy an evening

paper and had ended up buying comics and sweets at the same time, and as the hospital was only a few minutes' walk from the flat he went round there with them.

There was no slender blonde beside the bed and he didn't know whether to be glad or sorry. Josh told him that his mum had just left after being there all day, and that he was going home next morning.

'Good for you,' Kane said with one of his rare smiles. 'I'll bet your cousins are looking forward to seeing you again.'

'Those girls? The twins?' Josh said with boyish scorn. 'All they think about are their dolls.'

'And what is it with you?' Kane asked, hiding a smile. 'Footballs? Like the one you went on to the road for?'

Bright blue eyes refused to meet his.

'I know. I was stupid. I won't do it again.'

'I should think not. Watch what you're doing in future.'

As he got up to go Josh surprised him by saying, 'When will I see you again?'

He hesitated. This visit was just a one-off because the lad was in hospital and because he lived but a stone's throw away.

'I'm not sure,' he told him, ruffling the boy's fair locks. 'It depends on what your mother has to say.' And he went on his way, thinking that it might be quite a lot, with words like 'presumptuous' featuring prominently.

As Selina walked Josh across the village green to her brother's house early on Tuesday morning she was wondering if she'd done the right thing by agreeing that he could go to school.

He was getting around all right on crutches and in every other way was back to his normal self, but her confidence had been badly shaken by the accident and on Monday morning she'd been to see the headmaster.

It had transpired that the blame lay equally between Josh and the school. On his part because he'd unfastened the gate to get the ball, and on their part because the fastener on the gate hadn't been completely childproof. There had also only been one playground supervisor on duty instead of two.

'We admit that we are partly to blame, Mrs Sanderson,' the headmaster had said, 'but Joshua knew that he wasn't allowed to leave the school yard and…well…we both know what happened. He got carried away in the excitement of the moment and all he could think of was to retrieve the football.'

'What about the motorist?' she'd asked and the head had smiled.

'He was an elderly man passing through and, luckily for Joshua, a very cautious driver.'

She'd shuddered.

'Yes, indeed.'

And now, in half an hour's time, she would be back at the ambulance depot, and some time after that Jill would drop Josh off at school before taking the twins to their playgroup. And with Gavin already on his way to another day in Accident and Emergency, they would all be in their appointed places.

For some reason she was apprehensive about what the coming day might hold for her. She'd last seen Kane Kavener on Friday afternoon when he'd taken her home to change.

The circumstances under which they'd met weren't what she would have wished, but there was no putting the clock back. And they were going to be workmates, for heaven's sake! The best way to approach the coming meeting at the ambulance station was with pleasant, polite professionalism and see how that went down.

As soon as she walked into the staffroom behind where

the ambulances were garaged, Selina was surrounded by those going off duty and those coming on.

'How's the boy?'

'How's young Josh?'

Their concern brought a lump to her throat.

These were people who were seeing pain and sickness every day of their lives, often in their more dire forms, and a degree of impersonality was the only way they could cope. But when it came to one of their own—and it was Selina, who had already had one awful tragedy to cope with—they were right behind her.

She was aware that Kane was on the perimeter of the group around her, standing to one side, aloof and silent as if he didn't belong, but when their eyes met he smiled.

It wasn't on a par with the morning sun, more a relaxing of the face muscles, but at least it was a welcome of sorts, and with a feeling that it was going to be a very interesting day she helped herself to a mug of hot tea and waited for him to make the first move.

He didn't have to. She'd barely put the drink to her lips when the station officer appeared and beckoned her over.

'I believe you've already met Kane Kavener, who is to replace Charlie Vaughan,' fifty-year-old Mark Guthrie said. 'You will partner him as you did Charlie…and, Selina, make him welcome. He's a newcomer to the unit and a stranger in our town, and you know how keen I am to have harmony amongst the staff.

'A couple of the other guys would have liked you to be partnering them, though I can't think why,' he went on, with a twinkle in eyes that could be as bleak as a winter day when things went wrong. 'But Kane is here as Charlie's replacement and you were his partner.'

The twinkle was still there as he said, 'It's not always wise to let you folks have all your own way. So just to be awkward I'm putting you with the one who isn't too keen on working with a woman, and those who are bursting to turn out with you remain as before.'

There was a troubled frown on her face.

'I don't want to be an object of distrust...or desire. All I want is to do the job to the best of my ability and then go home to my son.' Her voice was flat. 'So Kane is putting up with me on sufferance? What's he got against woman-kind?'

'Probably nothing. He came with excellent references. Was a top performer at his last place. So perhaps—'

'He thinks that the casualties we collect won't be the only passengers?' she said tightly.

'I don't know. But if he does, you'll have to show him how wrong he is, won't you?'

'Yes, won't I?' she agreed, and as Mark departed for the inner sanctum of his office Selina went to face the day with a man she had been prepared to like but now wasn't so sure.

But he *had* taken the trouble to visit Josh in the hospital and she couldn't let it pass without thanking him. So as he turned away from the refreshment counter where he'd been chatting with Olga, the tealady, she said, 'It was good of you to go to see Josh on Saturday night. He's short of male company.'

That would let him see that even if he was sexist, she wasn't. But then he wouldn't know that Mark had just spilled the beans about him preferring a male partner.

'It was my pleasure,' he said easily. 'I'm renting a flat that's only minutes away from the hospital.'

'And have you settled in all right?'

He grimaced. 'It's not exactly from the *Better Homes Guide*, but because of coming down here at the last minute I took the first thing I was offered. However, in the near future I shall be looking to change my habitat, maybe to somewhere in the vicinity of your delightful village.'

Long-lashed violet eyes observed him in surprise. That might have been nice to know if it hadn't been for the fact that he wasn't keen to work with her.

'I'm sure you'll find somewhere,' she said casually. 'Not everyone can settle into country life.'

It was his turn to stare. So that was it, he thought. She might have to put up with him workwise, but she didn't want her home territory invaded.

Their first call of the day came through at that moment, putting an end to the stilted conversation. Kane was already moving, with Selina right behind him.

One ambulance had already gone out while Mark Guthrie had been talking to her and now it was their turn.

As they left the canteen Kane pressed the button to activate the machinery that would raise the heavy metal exit doors, and once they'd climbed aboard they were off within seconds.

They were allowed eight minutes to arrive at the scene of the emergency and by that time would have discovered from information received on the computer in the cab what degree of urgency there was in the request for an ambulance.

The most urgent, like heart attacks or chest pains that might lead to cardiac arrest or the sudden onset of other life-threatening illnesses, along with serious traffic accidents or major catastrophes, were classed as red alerts.

Less serious-sounding accidents, inside and outside the home, were amber alerts, and anything not so urgent, yet requiring the service of am ambulance, were logged as green.

Being prewarned about the seriousness of the incident that they were approaching gave the crews the chance to prepare themselves for whatever lay ahead.

Obviously there were times when a red alert had become amber or even green by the time they got there, or vice versa, but in the main the system worked for both paramedics and patients.

The one they were speeding towards had a seriousness all of its own—a house fire on an estate on the outskirts of the city.

Fire Services were already there and the ground floor of the property was well alight according to the message received at the ambulance station.

Selina had attended fires before with Charlie, and his calm skills had helped combat the horror of what they'd found awaiting them in many instances.

But today another man was in charge, an unknown quantity, and she hoped he was going to be as efficient as his predecessor.

'Have you been out to a fire before?' Kane asked crisply as she sat beside him in the passenger seat, deep in thought.

'Yes. I've been to a few,' she said quietly.

'Any fatalities?'

'Some.'

'Not pleasant.'

'No. Certainly not!' she agreed with a shudder and a quick glance at his unrevealing profile.

Was this how it was going to be? Selina wondered. Staccato sentences, fired at her like bullets. Was it the moment to tell him that she'd heard he didn't like working with women, and if that was so, it was just too bad as up to now *she* wasn't over the moon with jovial Charlie's replacement?

But the comment had come to her secondhand and Selina believed in making her own judgements. Kane had been kind to Josh and herself on two occasions when he'd barely known them, so what it was going to be like working with him was a matter of wait and see.

There was just one casualty, she was relieved to see—a

man with burns to the arm and chest. The remains of a sweater of some sort were hanging loosely around him.

He was sitting on the grass verge outside the house while firemen were round the back, tackling the kitchen, which was burning fiercely.

It appeared that he was a night worker who had decided to make himself a meal when he'd got in at seven o'clock that morning. But tired after a long shift, he'd fallen asleep with the chip pan on and had only awakened when the kitchen had been ablaze.

He'd suffered what looked like second-degree burns as he'd tried to put out the fire, but on seeing that it was too widespread he'd run outside only just in time.

'The wife's at work,' he croaked as they helped him into the ambulance. 'She'll never forgive me for this. I've burnt the house down and frizzled myself, all because I fancied some chips.'

'She might just be glad that you're alive,' Selina said as Kane opened the water-gel kit they carried for emergencies such as this.

It was a big moist blanket made to cover burns, with a twofold purpose. It stopped the skin from drying and tightening and kept the air away from tissue that had been exposed in the fire.

Kane had said little, leaving Selina to offer what consolation she could, but he'd displayed a sort of speedy efficiency that had immediately made her think that Charlie must have slowed down somewhat in latter years.

Here was a man who was really into the job, she thought. It was the kind of call-out that she'd taken part in on many occasions, but with Kane it felt different. He was confident and obviously very experienced, so the fact that he wasn't into the usual chit-chat didn't really matter.

By the time they arrived at Accident and Emergency the

burns victim was having rigors and Kane eyed him in quick concern.

'He's in shock and becoming dehydrated,' he said as he leapt out of the ambulance. 'Let's get him in there fast, Selina.'

When they'd delivered the patient to the A and E staff and were about to return to the unit, Kane said, 'I noticed that your doctor friend isn't on today.'

It was said casually, but she couldn't help but feel that there was a reason behind the comment, and when she said with equal nonchalance, 'Gavin isn't my "doctor friend", he's my brother,' he actually smiled.

'Oh, I see. I thought it was handy if you had a boyfriend in A and E. Prompt attention and all that.'

'I haven't got a boyfriend anywhere,' she said stiffly. 'I have a child to care for, a house to run and a very demanding job, all of which leave me very little time for socialising. I lost my husband just twelve months ago, which isn't a very long time in which to be thinking of replacing him.'

When the words were out Selina wished she'd been struck dumb before uttering them. Why was she justifying herself to this taciturn stranger? Was it because she felt that she had to make a stance? Clarify her position? Or was it because he had evoked anger in her with his tactless remark?

Kane could be excused for not knowing that Gavin was her brother, but as for the rest of it… Had he been given cause somewhere along the line to think that her sex couldn't manage without a man?

'I'm sorry,' he said abruptly. 'I didn't mean to offend you and will bear your comments in mind.'

Selina groaned inwardly. Now he was making it look as if she was warning him off. As if she thought that every man she met saw an attractive young widow as easy prey.

Selina had no need to worry about *him*, Kane was thinking. He'd had enough aggro to last him a lifetime with the Eve Richards business. He was only just beginning to come up for air now that the taint had been removed.

If the first call-out they'd dealt with together had gone smoothly, it wasn't to be so with the second. Before they'd got back to base another red alert came through on the dashboard computer.

A child was choking with a foreign object stuck in its throat at an address in a nearby avenue.

They were there within seconds, a flash of white shirts and navy trousers as they hurled themselves up the path with Kane in the lead and Selina following with the smaller of the two response bags.

The front door was already open and in a back sitting room a young mother was holding a small boy from behind. With her fists beneath his breastbone she was making frantic inward and upward thrusts to try to dislodge whatever it was that was choking him.

An agitated neighbour was hovering and when she saw them she cried, 'Help the bairn, for God's sake!'

He was blue in the face, eyes rolling in his head, and Selina knew that they only had seconds to free whatever it was.

'Dean swallowed a plastic toy and it's stuck,' the mother screamed at them, becoming hysterical now that help had arrived.

As Kane snapped, 'Forceps!' Selina already had them in her hand.

'Take him!' he ordered with the same brevity.

Obeying, she grabbed the child out of his mother's arms. As she did so he went limp.

'He's barely breathing!' she said in low voice.

Kane nodded. 'Lay him on the floor. As long as there's

some inhalation, however faint, I'm going to try to remove the toy before we start to resuscitate, otherwise we'll be defeating the object. If I can't get at it with the forceps I'll have to do a tracheostomy.'

They were both on their knees now, Selina behind the child's head and Kane at his side. As she held open the boy's slack mouth, he shone a pencil torch into his throat.

'Can you see it?' she asked.

He shook his head.

'No... Yes! Yes! I can! It's bright green and oblong.'

'Can you reach it?' she gasped.

'You bet I can,' he said coolly. 'Don't let the boy move, Selina. I don't want to push it further down than it is already.'

The only sound in the room was the sobbing of the distraught mother as Kane carefully lifted the obstruction out of her child's throat. He held it aloft triumphantly, before throwing it to one side and ordering, 'Oxygen, Selina. He's still breathing but only just.'

An hour later they were back at the ambulance station. The little boy, with his relieved mother in attendance, had been admitted to the children's ward at the hospital, where they were going to examine his throat for any damage from the obstruction and would monitor his breathing for twenty-four hours.

It had been Selina's turn to be silent on the return journey and eventually he'd said, 'So what's the problem?'

'There isn't one.'

'Oh, come on!' he hooted. 'Let me guess. You don't like working with me. You prefer cheerful Charlie. You think I was too chatty with the boy's mother on the way to hospital. Or maybe the opposite—that I'm not sympathetic enough with the public.'

'You're crazy,' she said with a smile that took the sting

from the words. 'How can I know whether I like working with you? It's only our first day together. As to Charlie, you're faster than he was, but not as cheerful by any means.

'And, no, I didn't think you were too familiar with Dean's mother. You were just trying to calm her. I haven't had time to see how you treat the public in general, but it seems clear that you see me as a pair of hands rather than a person. Could that be because you don't like working with someone of my sex?'

He eyed her sharply at the question.

'And who might have told you that?'

'Does it matter?'

'No. I suppose not. But I'm not keen on having my likes and dislikes discussed in public.'

'So is it true?' she persisted.

'Yes and no.'

'Meaning?'

'I once had an unpleasant experience.'

'And have now tarred us all with the same brush?'

A smile tugged at the corners of Kane's fascinating mouth.

'You make me sound like a flattering combination of male chauvinist and bighead.'

Selina had to laugh.

'I'm sorry. I didn't mean to. It's early days for us, isn't it? We'll adjust to each other's peculiarities in time, no doubt.'

As Kane's cool, dark gaze took in the charms of his new assistant he knew that he didn't find her peculiar at all. Unique maybe. She was beautiful in her golden slenderness, and tranquil with it, unlike a lot of women he'd come across.

Yet life had dealt her a poor hand so far. She'd lost a young husband and it stood to reason that they'd been happy. He couldn't imagine a man being unhappy with a woman like Selina Sanderson.

He shook his head as if to clear it. He was getting soft, rhapsodising over a woman he'd only just met. And wasn't he supposed to be watching his step as far as her sex were concerned?

When they arrived back at the station Selina said, 'Let's go and grab a coffee before we're called out again.'

'Good idea,' he agreed equably, and it was as if their challenging discussion on the way back had never been.

During the next few days they established a situation they both seemed reasonably happy with. Workwise Selina was aware that Kane was extremely efficient, and under his brisk command they were offering a first-class service to sick and injured alike.

From a personal point of view she was curious about him. He hadn't said so in so many words, but from the odd comment he'd made and his attitude in general she deduced that he had no ties, which was surprising as he was of striking appearance. Not attractive or handsome in the true sense of the words, but with a sort of dark magnetism that would instinctively appeal to womankind in general.

He was the complete opposite of Dave. He'd been fair-skinned, with light brown hair and boyish good looks, and as she dwelt on the comparison Selina was aghast at the channels that her thoughts were moving along.

Since losing the man who'd been her childhood sweet-heart, no other male had invaded her consciousness until now. But, she told herself with calming reason, it was only to be expected that she would be aware of Kane if they were going to be working together for twelve hours at a time.

Charlie popped in for a chat and invited them all to join

him for a farewell drink at a bar close to the station, and most of those who weren't on duty agreed to go.

Selina and Kane were due for two days off and, knowing that Jill wouldn't mind having Josh for this one evening, she accepted the invitation.

Kane had said nothing, obviously feeling that as a new member of staff it didn't apply to him, but Charlie said, 'You, too, Kane, if you feel like joining us. It's no joke moving to a new town where you don't know anyone, is it?'

Kane smiled, giving nothing away as usual, and said easily, 'Thanks. I'll bear it in mind.'

Selina felt guilty after that. Charlie was right. Kane *was* alone in a strange town. The station officer had reminded her of that on that first day. Though she'd like to bet he wouldn't be alone for long.

At least she could offer him some hospitality until he'd made some friends. He'd said that he had a basic sort of flat somewhere near the hospital and that was all she knew about him.

'I'll be going to Charlie's farewell tomorrow night,' she said awkwardly as they set out on a call shortly after his visit, 'but I've nothing planned for the night after and I wondered if you would like to come round for a meal.'

She could feel her face warming as he observed her with surprised dark eyes.

'Just to show you some northern hospitality,' she said quickly, 'and I'm sure that Josh would like to see you again.'

'Really? Well, on the strength of that I can't refuse. What time?'

'Seven?'

'Yes, that will be fine.'

Later that night, sitting quietly in the summer twilight with Josh fast asleep upstairs, Selina was regretting her rash offer. Did she want another man eating at her table…in the house that had been hers and Dave's?

She didn't know whether she did or not, but she was about to find out. And, she reasoned, wasn't she making too much of it? She'd asked Kane to dine with them merely as a gesture to a stranger in their town, not as a date.

When she'd asked Jill if she would mind Josh while she went to Charlie's party her sister-in-law had said, 'But of course. It's time you had a social life. You haven't had an evening out since Dave—'

'I know,' Selina had agreed softly, 'and I haven't wanted one, but I'm fond of Charlie…and I might as well tell you I'll be socialising the night after, too, but here on my own patch.'

Jill's eyes had sparkled.

'Tell me more!'

'I've invited my new partner round for a meal. He doesn't know anyone in these parts and I thought I should show him some hospitality.'

'Well! How old is he? What's he like? Is he free?'

She had to laugh.

'Hold on! He's thirty-something. Darkly brooding. And I don't know whether he's free or not. That doesn't come into it. I'm merely being hospitable…nothing else.'

Jill had given her a quick hug.

'Yes, I know, my dearest one, but Gavin and I don't want you to be alone for ever. Dave would want you to—'

Selina put a gentle finger on her lips.

'I know what you're saying, but he would be a hard act to follow…and then there's Josh.'

'What about him?'

'He has to have a say in those sort of things.'

CHAPTER THREE

WHEN Selina walked into the bar in the city centre she felt suddenly awkward. It was the first time she'd been in such a place without Dave and she thought sadly that it was yet another occasion to remind her that she was a woman alone.

But surprise was wiping out her melancholy. Kane was standing by the bar and she caught her breath. It was the first time she'd seen him out of uniform and he was impressive. In a blue silk casual shirt and tailored trousers, he was the most attractive man in the place.

He was chatting to the barman as the man was measuring out a drinks order and it was only when Charlie cried, 'Selina! I'm glad you made it,' that he became aware of her presence.

He swivelled round slowly at the sound of the older man's greeting, and as their eyes met Selina felt her colour rise.

She'd dressed with care for this first social foray since Dave's death. For some reason it had seemed important to do so, like flying a flag of independence. As she'd surveyed herself before leaving the house she'd known that in a long skirt of soft cotton that swirled around her ankles in a swish of bright colour and a low-cut black evening top she was looking her best.

There was still the extreme slenderness about her that spoke of months of stress and sorrow, but she was coming out of it slowly, turning towards the light again, and as always there was Josh. A bright candle in the gloom.

This wanting to look her best couldn't have anything to

do with Kane she assured herself. For one thing, she hadn't expected him to be there.

But you did know there was a possibility that he might turn up. The voice of conscience was teasing, and that made her cheeks burn even more.

He was coming across and she felt the need to get the first word in.

'This is a surprise. A pleasant one, too,' she said with a smile. 'It gives you the chance to get to know us all better and see something of the city besides the ambulance depot.'

Was it nerves that were making her so effusive? she wondered. Or was it true? That it *was* a pleasant surprise to see him there?

'And what about you, Selina?' he asked evenly. 'Is this sort of an evening a pleasure...or an ordeal?'

Her eyes widened. Surely he couldn't know what had been going through her mind.

'A bit of both, I think,' she said with a wry smile. Not wanting to elaborate on that, she strolled across to where the others were seated and Kane followed.

The bar management had put on an excellent buffet for the ambulance personnel at Charlie's request, and as the evening progressed Selina began to relax.

She'd been tense in those first few moments on arriving, but with the knowledge that Josh was safe and sound at Gavin's, and that those she was with all had in common their dedication to the ambulance service, she began to enjoy herself.

Another time she wouldn't feel so awkward. She'd broken down the barrier that her new and inescapable circumstances had put up and was feeling happier for it.

Having Kane beside her for most of the evening could have had something to do with it, but she wasn't prepared to delve deeply into that.

It was sufficient that his casual yet watchful gaze was

upon her whenever she felt the strangeness coming over her again and, although he didn't say much, his presence was oddly comforting.

'And so when are these new tactics being put into practice?' Charlie asked at one point in the evening.

There was silence as they all observed him in puzzlement.

'Ooops! Have I let the cat out of the bag?' He chuckled. 'Mark Guthrie was telling me about them when I called in at the station this afternoon. No doubt he'll be putting you all in the picture at the first opportunity but in the meantime I think I'd better keep quiet. I don't want to steal his thunder.'

'Aw, come on...tell us,' someone said, but the elderly ex-paramedic shook his head.

'No. Let the boss be the one to break the news.'

And with that they had to be satisfied.

It was close on midnight when the gathering broke up, and as Selina went to her car Kane was by her side.

'Is it still on for tomorrow night?' he asked as she started the car.

'Yes, of course,' she said quickly, with a sudden sinking feeling that she should have waited a while before asking him round for a meal.

He smiled.

'Right. I'll see you then. And, Selina, if there's time I'd love you to show me around your village.'

She smiled up at him from inside the car's dark interior, and as a group of rowdy revellers went by, followed by a police car with sirens blaring, she told him, 'Living there is heaven after experiencing what goes on out here.'

'Tell me about it!' he agreed sombrely. 'I'm not intending to stay where I am for long, that's for sure.'

With that he went striding off into the warm night, and Selina drove home with two thoughts uppermost in her mind. Was Kane thinking of moving to the village where she lived? And if he was, how would she feel about it?

Josh was staying at Gavin's for the night, and as she went slowly up the stairs in the quiet cottage for once she wasn't dreading the emptiness of the big double bed.

Selina was cool, calm, and collected the next night until Kane arrived with flowers and wine, and then she became flustered.

'Just to say thanks for inviting me,' he said easily, averting his gaze from her rosy cheeks.

Fortunately Josh was there to take their visitor's attention off her.

'You're my paramedic friend, aren't you?' he said. 'The one who brought me comics and sweets?'

Kane smiled down at him.

'Yes. That's me. What would you like us to do while your mother sees to the food?'

'Cricket. I've got a new bat.'

'And bails? We can't play without bails...and a corkie.'

Josh was already out on the garden path and beckoning Kane to follow him. 'Yes, I've got the lot. My dad used to play for the village team.'

Kane raised dark brows to show that he was suitably impressed and went on to ask, 'Was he a batter or a bowler?'

'Both,' Josh told him proudly, and Selina, listening to them through the kitchen window, felt the awkwardness that she'd experienced when he'd arrived disappear.

If Kane was a man of few words and cold efficiency while on the job, he was certainly putting himself out to be affable now, she thought thankfully.

But her face sobered as another thought came to mind. Was it because he was sorry for them...the bereaved? She hoped not. Pity was the last thing she would want from anyone, least of all this man.

He had walked across to the open window and seen her change of expression.

'Everything all right, Selina?'

'Yes, of course. I'll call you when I'm ready to serve.'

When they came in from the garden Josh was jubilant. 'I got Kane out for a duck, Mum,' he chortled.

'Yes. He did,' Kane agreed in mock dismay. 'Pity it wasn't a bit earlier. We could have had it for dinner.'

She was hoping that he'd forgotten his request to be shown the village, but when they'd eaten and she'd cleared away he said, 'And now for the conducted tour. Yes?'

Selina got reluctantly to her feet. Supposing Kane saw something he liked? There were a few properties for sale. Did she want him so near?

They saw enough of each other at the station without being under each other's feet while off duty, and he was in her thoughts enough already.

There were two places that she was going to avoid, but she hadn't reckoned with Josh.

'Let's go by the garage and see if Uncle Peter's there,' he suggested, 'and then go along the canal to the marina.'

It took Selina all her time not to groan out loud. Peter Abbot, who owned the local garage, was Dave's cousin and, like herself, was partnerless. His wife had left him, and because they were both on their own he'd been sending out signals that they should get together.

He was a likeable enough man, but the last person on earth that she would contemplate as anything but a friend. For one thing, his one topic of conversation was cars!

Hopefully the garage would be closed by now, but there was the Lock-Keeper's Cottage, situated close to the marina. It was a house that she'd always wanted to live in. Built of limestone with high apexes and mullioned win-

dows, it had a sort of compelling charm about it…and incredibly it was for sale. A fact that had registered only
briefly as there was no way that she could afford to buy it.
But what if Kane was wealthier than she?

The garage wasn't shut. Peter was working beneath a
silver Jaguar out on the forecourt and her spirits sank as
Josh ran over to him and tugged at his feet.

As he slid from under the car he looked across to where
they were standing a few feet away and then slowly pulled
himself upright.

'Selina!' he said, wiping his hands on an oily rag. 'This
is a pleasant surprise.'

As far as he took any notice of the man by her side Kane
could have been invisible, but she wasn't going to allow
that. Maybe here was an opportunity to let Peter see that
she wasn't as alone as he'd thought.

'Allow me to introduce Kane Kavener,' she said pleas-
antly. 'We work together on the ambulances.'

'How do you do?' Peter said stiffly. 'Been there long?'

'No. Just a short time,' Kane told him.

'Hmm. Right. Well, if you folks'll excuse me, I have to
get on. The customer's expecting this to be ready by morning.' And he eased himself back underneath the car.

'A relative?' Kane asked casually as they continued
along the village's main street. 'Josh referred to him as
"Uncle Peter".'

'My husband's cousin.'

'I see.'

He did see. He saw quite clearly, Kane thought as they
strolled along. That guy had a claim on her of some sort.
Or thought he had. And if that *was* the case, was it any of
his business?

When Selina had invited him to eat with them he'd been
surprised. For one thing, she didn't know him from Adam,

and for another it was plain to see that she was still grieving for her husband.

He supposed it was the hand of friendship to a stranger that she was offering and all credit to her for the thought. But he sensed that wasn't *all* it was.

Kane could tell that she thought he wanted to come and live in the village, and she was right. He did. It was an enchanting place. But he could also tell that she didn't want him to for some reason, and there was no way he would want to upset this fragile young widow.

So when they came to Lock-Keeper's Cottage, nestling beside the peaceful canal, with its 'for sale' board tantalisingly displayed, he concealed the excitement that was gripping him and walked casually past.

'That's the house where we'd like to live, isn't it, Mum?' Josh said guilelessly, and Selina managed a smile.

'Yes…in our dreams, Josh,' she said quietly, and that was that.

Driving back to the city, Kane was deep in thought. He'd enjoyed the evening more than he cared to admit. Young Josh was a great kid, and his mother…what was she?

A beautiful young woman whose flame was burning low. Maybe Josh was the only thing that was keeping it alight at all. Would she end up with the garage fellow? Probably. He'd seen a lot of cases where a widow had chosen a friend or relative of the dead man for a second husband.

Selina certainly wouldn't be interested in someone who'd been labelled a sex maniac. It was grossly untrue, but if she ever found out, how would she react? She might be prepared to give him the benefit of the doubt but, having done so, still find it distasteful to be associated with him.

As if it were only yesterday, he could still remember the nudge-nudge, wink-wink attitude of his male colleagues and the glacial stares of the women on the unit. All because of Eve Richards's desperate need for a man in her life.

And with regard to Selina, was he interested in a woman who already had a family? He was quite capable of providing his own offspring should he have the desire to do so, and in any case he valued his freedom.

As to that fantastic house by the canal, there would be other properties in other places that might appeal to him, without Selina Sanderson in the background, wondering what his motives were.

They were both back on duty the next day. As the night shift were getting ready to depart and the day shift were arriving Mark Guthrie called them all together.

'Due to government funding, in a week's time we are to start a new 999 system that will make our response time even quicker,' he said, meeting their curious glances. 'The money that has been allocated to us will be spent on extra paramedics and ambulances, and a dozen fast-response vehicles each manned by one person only. These white estate cars will go out in the first instance to many of the emergencies, but they won't have the facilities for taking anyone to hospital. The ambulance that follows them will do that if required.

'That is one side of the strategy. The other is that, instead of ambulances being called out from base, crews will be stationed at black spots—in other words, the areas where the most calls come from.'

'These so called black spots will be chosen with facilities for washing and eating being available for our personnel while they are waiting to be called out, and if we find that one area is busier than another we'll reschedule our resources accordingly.'

He paused, then asked briefly, 'Any questions?'

'Yes. I have one,' Kane said. 'Where will those manning

the fast-response vehicles be recruited from? Amongst ourselves? Or will they be new staff?'

'Some of both,' Mark said. 'The positions will be more stressful, carrying more responsibility, and those involved will work shorter hours because of those factors. Why?' he went on. 'Are you interested in applying yourself?'

Selina was surprised to find that she was holding her breath. They'd only just teamed up. If Kane went on one of the fast-response vehicles she would see little of him. Even more surprising was the thought that she didn't want that to happen.

'No. Not at the moment,' the man on her mind said levelly, 'but I think it only fair that we should all be clear as to what options we have.'

The station officer nodded.

'I agree. Anyone who has any queries about the new structure can refer to the notice that will be going up on the board shortly. Alternatively, they can come to see me.

'In closing I want to say that our city is aiming to make what is already an efficient service even better, and having extra staff and vehicles will certainly help to accomplish that.'

As they took their first call of the day a little later Selina said, 'I would have thought working on your own would have appealed to you.'

They were speeding to the scene of a motorcycle accident and he didn't take his eyes off the road as he said, 'Who says it doesn't?'

'So?' she persisted. 'Why did you tell Mark that you weren't going to apply? It would solve the problem of having to work with me…a woman.'

'Have I complained?'

'Er…no. But I get the feeling that you're not over the moon at the arrangement.'

'The only time I would express my doubts about the set-up would be if I found that you weren't competent, and from what I've seen that isn't likely to happen. Or maybe if you started coming on to me.'

'Coming on to you?' she gasped. 'If that means what I think it does, you have some nerve! You're just like the rest of the male population…under the impression that having lost one husband, I'm on the lookout for another…or the equivalent. I've already had two offers to "fulfil my needs" from guys I've met in the course of the job…and they were married! And as to those who aren't, I would expect them to run a mile from a widow with a child.'

Her voice broke on a sob and he flinched.

'It's not like that,' she choked. 'I just want to be left alone.'

Kane bit into his bottom lip with even white teeth. If he'd wanted to break through Selina's reserve, what better way could he have found? But what a fool he'd been to make such a comment!

He'd made it sound as if he thought he was God's gift to women when, if the truth be known, he'd felt anything but desirable with the stigma of recent events upon him.

The nightmare of working with Eve Richards had been in his mind when he'd said what he had, but Selina knew nothing about that. She didn't know what it was like to have to watch every word or gesture in case it could be used as part of a disturbed mind's fabrications.

Maybe it was just as well that for different reasons they both had no desire to get involved, but now, somehow or other, he had to make amends for his insensitivity.

He reached out and took her clenched fist in his big, capable hand.

'I'm sorry, Selina. I spoke without thinking about your situation. It's just that in the past I've been propositioned a few times and, well, I don't like it. So, please, dry your eyes and tell me that I'm forgiven for being an insensitive clod.'

She threw him a watery smile.

'You're forgiven. I'm afraid that I'm very touchy these days. And, Kane?'

'What?'

'I'm not surprised that you've had to fight them off.'

'Really? Well, the same applies to you. It's no wonder that you're seen as an attractive and available commodity in the world of relationships. And as to those who are already married, they're just lusting cheats.'

She was laughing now.

'We are something else, you and I. One moment we're at each other's throats and the next we're a mutual admiration society.'

Yes, indeed, he thought wryly, but there wouldn't be much admiration going around if she knew all there was to know about him.

A young motorcyclist was lying beside his overturned bike when they reached the scene.

'Seems that he swerved to avoid a child that had run into the road and hit the lamppost,' a police sergeant told them as the WPC who was attending the injured man moved to let them get near.

He was moaning faintly, his face white beneath his crash helmet, which was miraculously still in position. The policewoman had opened the front of his leathers and a huge blood stain was spreading across his shirt.

As Selina started to cut the garment away, the man made a choking sound and Kane said swiftly, 'Sounds as if his tongue's gone back.' Without further comment he pulled the man's slack jaws apart and, sure enough, the throat was blocked with the tongue which had flipped backwards with the force of the impact.

Part of the standard equipment carried by the ambulance

was a laryngoscope. With it he lifted the biker's tongue and brought it forward. Immediately the man's breathing improved. Then Kane turned his attention to the gaping stomach wound that Selina had uncovered.

'There's a lot of blood loss here,' he said crisply. 'We need to move him fast. We'll use the scoop stretcher for this one as I suspect there are fractures as well and I don't fancy sliding him onto a backboard with that sort of stomach damage.

'You drive,' he continued, 'while I try to stem the blood. And radio ahead to say that we're bringing in a red alert with a serious stomach injury.'

When Selina had passed the message on via the computer Kane nodded grimly and said, 'At best this guy is going to need an infusion of saline solution to counteract the blood loss, and at the worst a transfusion...amongst other things.'

The accident victim was lapsing in and out of consciousness and as they raced to the nearest hospital Selina was praying that they would get there in time.

The biker had been admitted and they were on their way back to base. An emergency team had been waiting to receive him and the treatment Kane had envisaged was being carried out, along with a CT scan to identify the extent of the stomach injury.

'He'll live, Selina,' Kane said as he observed her anxious expression. 'He's got youth and fitness on his side...and the best A and E team for miles around attending to him.'

'Yes, I know,' she said sombrely, 'but these are the times when I want to follow it through. The trouble with our job is that we're only in at the beginning. We rarely find out what happens to the patient in the end.'

'True,' he agreed, 'but we are there at the most important

time for a lot of people. Console yourself with that thought.'

But still in pensive mood, she asked, 'How long did it take us to get to him?'

'Ten minutes? Twelve at the most.'

'We're supposed to be there in eight.'

'We have to allow for heavy traffic. The roads were very busy.'

She nodded her head and the neat, golden ponytail moved with it.

'Yes, I know, but he could have died before we got there.'

'He could,' Kane agreed, 'but he didn't, did he? With the new system we should improve on our response times.'

'But supposing they have us positioned in the wrong place? It could take even longer,' she persisted doubtfully.

'No. I don't think so,' he said decisively. 'There'll be more of us, don't forget, and they can radio through to move us around if they've miscalculated where the accident black spots are.'

There was another thing about the new system that Selina wasn't sure about, but she wasn't going to bring that into the open.

When they were waiting to be called out at the ambulance station there were lots of other people around—paramedics, trainees, mechanics, snack-bar attendants and suchlike, along with the station officer, who left his office occasionally to check on what was happening.

With the new arrangements it would be different. She and Kane would be more isolated, just the two of them waiting for the call. What would they do during the quiet periods? What would they talk about? Would her awareness of him increase to such a degree that she couldn't get him out of her mind?

It wasn't far off that state of affairs already. Which just

went to show that she could still feel the kind of chemistry that ignited between the sexes.

As they drove past a mediocre apartment block in the city centre Kane said with a grim humour, 'That's where my palatial apartment is. I'd invite you in for coffee but the cups have all got cracks in them.'

'It sounds as if you really do need to move to somewhere better,' she said. 'Have you anywhere in mind?'

'Mmm,' he murmured. 'But there are problems.'

He received a quick slanting glance from violet eyes.

'Such as?'

'The location, for one thing.'

She knew then that she didn't want to know. If he told her that he wanted to move into the village, she would have concerns about them being too near...too disturbingly near.

Yet she didn't own the place and why should she begrudge this man, who seemed so much of a lone entity, the chance of enjoying the same country paradise as herself?

So she said nothing and Kane didn't pursue the subject. He just sat looking straight ahead until the big metal doors of the ambulance station lifted for them to enter.

Two weeks later the new system was functioning. There were two extra ambulances in the depot and staff numbers had increased accordingly to include an attractive, russet-haired paramedic by the name of Denise Hapgood.

In a short space of time she made it known that she was unattached and open to offers, and Selina noticed that when such comments were made the newcomer's glance was always on Kane.

But he might have been deaf for all the notice he took, and Selina had to admit to herself that she was relieved. Maybe he really was loth to be involved with women on the job. Yet he seemed to have accepted her as his partner and it did occur to her on several occasions that he perhaps saw her as a safe option, with widowhood newly upon her and a young son to care for.

Obviously something in the past had upset him with regard to the opposite sex and she would like to know what it was. He'd said that he'd been propositioned a few times. Whatever that meant. And she'd almost given the game away by telling him that she wasn't surprised.

She was attracted to Kane in spite of herself, and it wasn't just because of his looks. The dark short pelt of his hair and his chiselled features were memorable enough, but it was his eyes that had the biggest effect on her. They were deep hazel with golden flecks in them, sometimes guarded and inscrutable, at others warm and melting—but not very often.

It was irritating that she knew nothing about him. Whether he had family or friends. What he liked and disliked. Whether he was ambitious, eager to move up the healthcare ladder.

He was the type who would have made a good doctor, unflappable, clever, dedicated, but for some reason he'd chosen the ambulance service. One day she would ask him why.

She'd been right about the times when there were just the two of them waiting for the call to come. Sometimes they were half an hour sitting side by side as they waited for a message to flash up on the computer screen.

When it became too difficult to behave casually in his presence Selina made the excuse that she needed to freshen up or was gasping for a cup of tea. Anything to break out of the magical cocoon that wrapped itself around her every time she was with Kane.

If he was aware of her feelings, he didn't show it. He was cool and calm, and talked about everyday things mostly. He always asked after Josh. On one occasion when she happened to mention that the long school holidays would soon be upon them and, much as Jill and the girls loved having him, she felt it was a bit much, he surprised her by saying, 'So why don't we take the three little ones out on our days off? That would give your sister-in-law a break.'

'Are you sure?' she said hesitantly.

Was Kane really happy to be with three young children and a woman who was still hurting from what the fates had doled out to her and her husband?

It would seem that he was.

'Yes. I'm sure,' he said firmly. 'I wouldn't have suggested it if I wasn't.'

'That would be lovely, then,' she told him softly, and for the rest of the day there was a warm feeling around her heart.

On a warm afternoon in late July Selina felt her eyelids drooping as they sat in the cab of the ambulance. She'd been awake most of the night with Josh, who had a feverish cold, and now lack of sleep was taking its toll.

She'd been in a mad rush for the seven o'clock start as neither she nor Josh had wanted to get up when the time had come. Thankfully, as he'd climbed into her bed for a quick cuddle she'd discovered that his temperature had gone down and with the amazing resilience of childhood he'd almost been back to his normal self.

The last-minute and the subsequent weariness after a broken night had given a bad start to the day and she'd had little to say for herself.

Kane had eyed her questioningly a few times, but as no explanation of her lacklustre manner had been forthcoming he'd remained silent.

But now, as he watched her fighting off sleep, he thought he had the answer to her unaccustomed low spirits. She was tired. Was she sleeping badly? he wondered. Or sickening for something?

Being a single parent couldn't be easy. She looked young and defenceless as she slid over the edge into sleep and he reached across and took her hand in his. His touch brought a sleepy response and on the breath of a sigh she murmured her husband's name.

Kane flinched. Supposing she woke up suddenly and found they were holding hands? Especially after she'd been dreaming about Dave.

And supposing the station officer came along, as he sometimes did, to check them out. He wouldn't be pleased to find a member of his staff asleep on duty.

He knew that Selina trusted him to wake her up should they be needed. She wouldn't have gone to sleep otherwise, but someone else wouldn't see it like that.

'Selina,' he said softly. 'Wake up.'

'Mmm,' she murmured. Raising the hand that was holding hers, she pressed it gently against her cheek.

Kane groaned inwardly. She was in for a disappointment when she became really awake and found that it wasn't Dave sitting beside her.

Kane didn't know it, but he was assuming too much. Selina often said her husband's name as a reminder. She sometimes felt that the memory of him was slipping away and today had been one of those occasions. It hadn't meant that she'd been dreaming about him and she wasn't really asleep.

It would never do to let that happen on the job. They had to be alert and ready for those who needed them. But she hadn't been able to resist closing her eyes and slipping away for a few seconds.

When Kane had taken her hand in his she'd felt her pulses leap and had become wide awake at the same time.

But unable to resist seeing what he might do next, she'd feigned sleep.

However, the hand that she was holding against her cheek was being slowly withdrawn and she didn't want that to happen. There was something about his touch that was different from anything she'd ever experienced before, and she wanted more.

Her eyes flew open and met his and she saw consternation in them. He was pursing his lips in dismay and she knew why when he said, 'I'm sorry. I didn't mean to intrude into your thoughts about your husband. You looked tired and forlorn and I just wanted you to know that I was there.'

Selina looked down at the floor of the ambulance. She didn't know what to say. If she told him she hadn't been thinking about Dave it would make his solicitous explanation seem unwanted. And if she were to tell him that *he* was the one who'd been on her mind, that she was so aware of him she couldn't think straight, what would he do then?

She didn't know...and she wasn't going to risk finding out. If he repulsed her, she would want to die. So she said quietly and truthfully, 'Thanks for that, Kane. I try to keep his memory alive as best I can.'

CHAPTER FOUR

THAT evening Selina had a succession of callers.

Charlie Vaughan arrived first, and when she opened the door she felt a rush of pleasure. As they chatted amicably while Josh played in the garden, it was clear to see that the elderly paramedic was enjoying his retirement. Fishing and bowling on the green in the park seemed to take up a lot of his time, but he still wanted to know all about what was going on at the ambulance depot.

'How's the new system working out?' was his first question.

'All right, I think,' Selina told him.

'It will throw the crews together a lot more,' he said. 'How do you feel about that?'

'Fine,' she said easily. 'Why do you ask?'

'No reason. I just wondered how you were getting on with this new fellow.'

'Kane? No problem.'

'He's a bit of a loner, I'm told.'

'Er...yes, I suppose so,' she agreed hesitantly. 'That is, if you mean that he's not married...or with anyone.'

'The guys at the station were saying that one of the new women is after him.'

Selina swallowed.

'Possibly. I don't really know.'

'She might find that she's taken on more than she can handle with that one,' he said drily.

'Are you trying to tell me something or what?' she asked quickly. 'As far as I'm concerned, Kane is just someone I work with.'

His frown disappeared as if by magic and she observed him thoughtfully. Charlie knew something about Kane... but didn't want to tell her.

What was it? That he was the local rapist? That he'd robbed a bank? Or was he an infiltrator from the Ministry of Health? He was as likely to be a man from Mars as any of those things, and in any case, whatever it was, she didn't want to know.

She hated tittle-tattle and was prepared to take Kane as she found him. He was efficient, hardworking and thought-ful in lots of ways. His suggestion that they take the three children out during school holidays to give Jill a rest had been an example of that.

When Charlie had gone she couldn't settle. There was nothing worse than someone dropping hints without telling the full story. If she'd encouraged him to do so, he probably would have done, but her feelings for Kane were too new, too much like tender shoots springing up after a dark win-ter, and she couldn't bear the thought of them being tram-pled on.

Peter arrived just as Charlie was leaving, and as Selina stood at the gate to watch him drive off, Charlie wound down the car window and said in a low voice, 'Solid young fellow, that Peter. Just the type to look after you and Josh.'

Selina glared at him. *She* would be the judge of that!

'So?' Dave's cousin said when she went back inside. 'What have you been up to lately?'

'Nothing special,' she told him. 'With Josh to look after, the job and the house to see to, there aren't enough hours in the day. What about you?'

'Same here,' he grunted. 'But that doesn't mean I haven't got time for you, Selina. What about it, eh?'

She became very still.

'What about what?'

'Us getting married. I'm the next best thing to Dave.'

Oh, no, you're not! she thought angrily.

Dave had been Dave. He'd been special and she'd loved him a lot. There wouldn't ever be anyone like him and she certainly didn't want to settle down with a pale imitation in the form of his cousin.

If she ever fell in love again it would be for the man himself. Not because he smiled like Dave, made love like Dave, but because he was special in his own way.

And with that thought her mind went back to those moments in the ambulance earlier in the day when Kane had held her hand, thinking she was asleep, and had drawn back when he'd found that she hadn't been.

She had wanted the moment to go on. She'd wanted him to hold her close. Not in lust or quick passion, but so that she could feel his quiet strength and breathe in the clean male smell of him.

'So, what do you think?' Peter was asking, his flat tones breaking into her thoughts.

What did she think?

She thought that he'd asked her to marry him in the same tone that he might have asked a customer if they wanted two-stroke or diesel…and as his eyes went over her consideringly she thought angrily that the next thing he would be commenting on would be her chassis!

'I can't believe that I've heard you right,' she told him quietly. 'And if you think you're doing me a favour by asking me to marry you, forget it, Peter. At the present time I'm not intending to marry anyone.'

He scowled at her. 'What about the fellow that was with you that night? Where does he fit into the picture?'

Selina's eyes widened. First it had been Charlie with his innuendos and now Peter was dragging Kane's name into the conversation. What was the matter with them, for heaven's sake?

He would hate being discussed like this. Of that she was

sure. And so, instead of admitting that Kane was beginning to fit into the picture very nicely, she told her unwanted suitor what she'd told Charlie. 'Kane Kavener is just someone I work with. Just leave him out of it, will you?'

Peter got to his feet. 'Huh!' he snorted. 'Time will tell!' And with that he stomped off.

The last caller was her brother. Jill had sent Gavin round to ask if she could borrow a cake tin, and as they chatted about the day's events she began to relax.

This time it was her own doing that Kane's name was mentioned. Selina was aware that her voice sounded stilted as she said, 'Kane and I are going to take Josh and your girls out whenever we can during the school holidays to give Jill a break, if that's all right with you.'

Gavin laughed. 'Of course it is. Wait until I tell her!' His face sobered suddenly. 'What's this about Kane, then? He's the guy you work with, isn't he?'

'Mmm.'

'So just how friendly are you, sis? You know that Jill and I would love to see you with someone who'll take care of you, but just how well do you know him?'

She averted her eyes at the question and said, 'It's just a matter of weeks since he came onto the unit so I haven't known him long at all, but in any case it's not like that. It's just that he's alone in a strange town, and I was saying that I feel it's a bit much for Jill to have the three children all through the school holidays, apart from my days off. It was then that he suggested that we make up a fivesome.'

'Sounds great!' Gavin enthused. 'Next time he's out this way, bring him round for a drink.'

'Er…yes. I will.'

When he'd gone she went slowly up to bed. What a night! Charlie with his mysterious hints, Peter with his insulting proposal and then Gavin, sane, reasonable and understanding.

All men in her life to some extent, but it was Kane she thought of in those last seconds before sleep claimed her.

In his high-rise apartment amongst the city's rooftops Kane wasn't finding sleep as easy to come by.

He'd been to view the house by the lock during the evening and had been thinking about it ever since. He'd known instinctively that he would like it, both inside and out, before he'd even seen it, and he hadn't been wrong. However, the knowledge hadn't brought much pleasure with it.

For one thing, he'd vowed that he would look elsewhere for a property in the light of Selina's lack of enthusiasm every time he said how much he liked the village.

And for another, who had he seen arriving at her cottage as he'd driven past on his way home? The fellow from the garage. The one who'd looked him over with a jaundiced eye that night when she'd been showing him around the place.

He'd stopped at the end of the road and sat hunched behind the wheel of his car as he'd reasoned that Selina would have known the mechanic for ages. Hadn't she said he was a relative of some sort? She was bound to feel safe with someone like that.

Whereas he was…what? An unknown quantity. Someone who'd had his share of relationships with the opposite sex, but had always kept them light.

But with Selina it was different. He'd never met a woman who aroused such tenderness in him as she did. But there wasn't only the garage fellow to compete with. There was the memory of Dave. It had been his name on her lips when they'd been together in the ambulance that afternoon.

He would forget about the lockside cottage, he decided as a clock somewhere chimed the hour. He could afford to buy it, but for once being on his own didn't have its usual appeal.

And with Selina he needed to cool down. He'd always gone in for no strings in his relationships, but she was a woman with a cherished past, plus one small boy who just might not want a father substitute.

Unaware of Kane's gloomy deliberations of the night before, Selina turned up for work the next morning to find him deep in conversation with Denise.

The newcomer to the unit was smiling up at him provocatively and Selina thought glumly that if Kane were to become interested in that one they would be starting off equally. Denise had made it clear to anyone who might be interested that she was free of entanglements.

And what was she? A young widow with a child—an adorable child at that, but still an extra person in a new marriage.

He raised his hand in salute when he saw her, but instead of coming over called across casually, 'Morning, Selina. All right?'

'Yes, thanks,' she said brightly, and made her way to the rest room.

A new marriage! A voice inside her head scolded. You're jumping ahead a bit, aren't you? You're supposed to have accepted your lot.

She had, she admitted wryly, but that had been before she'd met Kane Kavener. Had meeting her affected him in the same way? she wondered. She doubted it. It would seem that he saw her mainly as an object for concern.

If only he knew how much she wanted to laugh and be happy, to be told that she was beautiful and desirable. She'd been sad for so long, drained with the worry of Dave's illness and the huge burden of care that it had brought with it. But now, although the grief and pain were still there, they were levelling out because there was no other course open to her but to accept that he was gone.

*   *   *

Today they had been told to position the ambulance in the city centre. The traffic was heavy there, amongst huge apartment blocks occupied mainly by business people. The area was an accident black spot and, sure enough, within minutes of their arrival they had proof of it.

An elderly man, too impatient to wait until the lights were green, had set off across a busy thoroughfare and been knocked down by an unprepared motorist.

When the message came up on the screen that there was a red alert nearby, Kane let the clutch in and said calmly, 'Here we go, Selina. Why is it that those with the most time on their hands are so impatient?'

It was the first comment he'd addressed to her since they'd climbed aboard and she'd been beginning to wonder if she'd upset him in some way or if he was still mesmerised by the charms of Denise. Whatever it was, there was a reserve about him today that was different from his usual calm reticence, and she wished she knew the cause of it.

The accident victim was lying unconscious in the middle of a pelican crossing and as the police, who had been first on the scene, diverted the traffic Selina and Kane knelt beside him.

It looked as if he'd gone head first when the car had hit him. A soft, squelchy mass above his right ear indicated that there might be bleeding within the skull.

'Check for fractures,' Kane said as he monitored the man's shallow breathing. 'He must have been hit with some force. Why couldn't he have waited, for goodness' sake?'

'The bones of the right arm and leg are out of alignment,' Selina told him as she cut away his clothes. 'It would seem that he took all the impact on his right hand side.'

'Mmm,' he murmured. 'We'd best lift him onto a backboard in case there are spinal injuries, but first let's get him splinted.'

As they raced to Accident and Emergency at the nearest of the big city hospitals Selina was driving while Kane kept a close watch on the patient. It was important to keep the airways clear, check the pulse and heartbeat and keep him warm as he began to go into shock.

Selina had sent a message ahead to say that they were bringing in a seriously injured road accident victim, and as the ambulance pulled up on the hospital forecourt the A and E staff were waiting to take over.

On the way back to their vantage point in the city centre she said flatly, 'So what have I done?'

Kane was in the driving seat this time. Without taking his glance off the road, he said, 'I'm not with you, Selina.'

'I think you are,' she continued in the same flat tone, 'but maybe aren't prepared to say what's bugging you.'

'I don't see why I should have to account for my mood swings to you,' he countered irritably. 'We're just colleagues, for heaven's sake!'

Selina felt her face grow warm. The last thing she'd intended had been to sound predatory. Kane had put her well and truly in her place and it caused a dull ache inside her.

They'd been getting on so well, or so she'd thought, but now he was making it clear that just because the job threw them together, it didn't mean they had anything else in common.

Had it only taken five minutes at the receiving end of Denise's predatory ways to make him so remote? she asked herself as the hurt increased. It looked like it.

'I'm sorry,' she said with a quiet gravity that made him want to reach out for her and hold her close. 'It was just that I thought I'd offended you in some way.'

'You haven't,' he said brusquely. 'I'm just a bit out of sorts, that's all. I think it must be that vile apartment. I must sort something out soon.'

He wasn't going to tell her that he'd already found somewhere that he would like to live but that it was almost on her doorstep and he wasn't sure how she would feel about that. Especially with the mechanic hovering, he thought ruefully. The role of gooseberry wasn't his style.

But neither could he let his enchanting assistant carry on thinking she'd upset him for some reason. She *had* upset him, but it had been through no fault of hers.

He'd always been quick to put on the brakes when a relationship was getting too serious and it had never bothered him, but Selina was different and she couldn't help being the woman she was. No more than she could help losing the husband she'd loved.

All this agonising and they weren't even in a relationship, he thought sombrely. Probably never would be. The only contact they'd had after spending hours in close proximity in the ambulance had been when he'd held her hand the day before.

'Don't take any notice of me, Selina,' he said. 'I can be a miserable blighter at times. If it's not the past creeping up on me, it's the present throwing me off course.'

She smiled and his gaze lingered on her mouth and the soft line of her throat.

'I haven't a clue what you mean by all that,' she said with a lift to her voice, 'but I'm happy as long as it's nothing I've done. I find working with you stimulating, Kane. Charlie was great, but with you, well…'

Her voice trailed off. She meant every word, but too much enthusiasm might be wrongly interpreted and she didn't want him to think she was like Denise.

Another call was coming through—a suspected heart attack victim in a nearby penthouse. That brought the strange conversation to a close.

It was the last week of July and Josh was totally happy. For one thing he was due to have his plaster cast off, and for another the long summer break from school was about to commence.

Kane hadn't mentioned them taking the three children out since that first time and, much as the idea appealed to her, Selina had no intention of reminding him.

Denise was monopolising him whenever she got the chance during working hours, and the last thing Selina wanted was to be seen as begging for his company.

Whether he saw the other woman away from the job she didn't know. It was his business if he did. He'd already made it clear that when it came to herself they were just colleagues in healthcare.

In the long, lonely months after losing Dave she had never given a thought to falling in love again. There had been Josh to think about…and the job…and the house… and her devastated father-in-law.

Gavin and Jill had been her lifeline. Always there when she'd needed them, but ready to step back when she wanted to be alone.

Dave's mother had died long ago, but his father was in excellent health and sadly it had been that fact that he hadn't been able to cope with as he'd watched his only son become weaker with each passing day.

'Why isn't it me lying there?' he'd groaned in bitter frustration, and Selina hadn't had an answer for him.

Now Robert Sanderson was retired and living in Devon. She and Josh had arranged to stay with him for two weeks of the holidays, but there would still be plenty of time left to take him and her two nieces out with Kane…if he hadn't changed his mind.

She was thinking about him far too much. The trim masculinity of him. The cool competence. The arresting face beneath thick dark hair, and the eyes, guarded and watchful whenever she was near.

Who was he, for heaven's sake? She knew nothing about

him except that he'd been working down south and then had moved up north for some reason.

She guessed him to be in his middle thirties, yet he seemed to have no ties of any kind. He hadn't mentioned parents or brothers and sisters, let alone wife or children.

Yet underneath it all she sensed calm strength and integrity and was becoming to feel that Kane Kavener had walked into her life for a reason.

'Be prepared for Josh to walk stiff-legged for a while,' Gavin told Selina when the plaster cast had been removed. 'Children are creatures of habit and he's had it on for quite some time. However, he'll soon be walking normally again. As you saw, the X-rays show that the leg has healed beautifully.

'How are you getting on with Kane?' he asked casually a little later as a delighted Josh preceded them slowly along the hospital corridor. 'From what I've seen of him, he's quite impressive.'

'He is,' she agreed with equal nonchalance.

'So you like him?'

They had always been close. She could tell Gavin anything, and before she changed her mind Selina said, 'Yes. I do. Too much for my own good, I feel.'

He put a brotherly arm around her shoulders and waited for her to go on.

'Am I being disloyal to Dave, Gavin? I never thought I'd ever want anyone else but him.'

He gave her a squeeze.

'Dave wouldn't mind. You're young and beautiful and still entitled to have a life. But what about Kavener? Is he attracted to you?'

'I don't think so. I thought he might be at first, but he's cooled off for some reason and someone else on the unit is already eyeing him up.'

She sighed. 'If a single man has a choice between two women, one with a child to bring up and the other as free and unfettered as himself, it's not hard to see which one he's going to choose, is it?'

'Aw, come on, Selina,' Gavin protested. 'It's quality that counts.' Before she could reply to that pearl of wisdom the bleeper in his top pocket was urging him back to the never-ending demands of A and E.

It was Saturday night and Selina was wishing Kane and herself on call anywhere other than in the city centre.

None of the squad liked Saturday night duty, but they all had to take their turn and tonight it was theirs. It was when it got to the early hours of Sunday morning that the problems started. When the rowdies and the legless came pouring out onto the streets from the clubs and bars.

The last time they'd been on duty they'd been called to a club where a young girl had been in a serious condition after taking ecstasy tablets and alcohol.

Selina had felt like weeping at the stupidity of her actions and Kane's face had been set in stone as they'd given her what treatment they could and had then driven to hospital with sirens screeching in the summer night.

They'd discovered afterwards that she'd survived, but with physical and mental damage that wouldn't easily be repaired. Selina was praying that there wouldn't be anything like that tonight.

There wasn't. But there were other incidents just as distressing.

A fight that had started in a queue at a taxi rank had resulted in one youth unconscious, having cracked his head on the pavement as he'd gone down, and another bleeding and battered, leaning against a shop window.

They were there before the police and as Selina and Kane leapt out of the ambulance the fight started up again. As they ran towards the unconscious victim a burly youth stepped back and knocked Selina off her feet.

The response bag that she was carrying went flying and the next thing she heard was Kane's voice, loud and furious, above the uproar.

'Stop it, you fools!' he bellowed. 'You've hurt my partner. You don't deserve our help if you're going to carry on like this!'

He was bending over her, his dark eyes full of concern and outrage, and she gasped, 'See to the injured, Kane. I'm all right.'

'You sure?' he asked tightly.

'Yes, I'm sure.' She got slowly to her feet.

She'd hurt her back, but it was hardly the moment to mention it, with two injured males and the rest of them still simmering, even though Kane's outburst had put an end to the scuffling.

The lad on the pavement was coming round. When he saw them hovering over him he croaked, 'They tried to push in front of us in the queue, and when we protested they got rough. Where's Tim?'

'I imagine that's him, over there,' Kane told him. 'It looks as if he's had some rough handling, too.' He glanced anxiously at Selina's pale face. 'Can you take over here while I see to the other guy?'

She nodded, hoping that he hadn't seen her wince.

'Yes. I'm fine.'

At that moment the police arrived and incredibly the street was suddenly empty, the only thing to be heard the sound of running feet.

'We'll get 'em,' a police sergeant told them grimly. 'We have helicopters up on Saturday nights. They'll follow them overheard and pick 'em out for us.'

Kane was only half listening. At that moment all he was concerned about was getting the injured to hospital and finding out from Selina if she was indeed as all right as she said she was.

Being involved in violent situations were all part of the job for both sexes, but he'd been staggered by the horror he'd felt when he'd seen Selina go down. If it hadn't been for the fact that they'd had two injured men to see to, he would have felt like sorting out the hooligans himself.

Why couldn't Selina have chosen a less dangerous and stressful career? he thought as she drove them through the breaking dawn. But you wouldn't have met her if that had been the case, he told himself soberly, and you wouldn't want that.

She looked tired and ethereal, as if a puff of wind would blow her away. Yet, tranquil as ever, she managed a smile when she found his gaze on her.

As he gave oxygen to one of the youths, who was having breathing difficulties, for the first time ever Kane wished himself far away from the sick and injured he was committed to save.

He wanted to take Selina away from the sordid and the stressful, to somewhere where he could show her the tenderness she aroused in him and tell her about the longing that made his loins ache.

When they'd delivered the two victims of the brawl into A and E, Selina said calmly, 'I'm going to have my back checked over before we leave, Kane. I jarred my spine when I fell.'

Alarm flickered in his eyes but she said smilingly, 'Don't panic. This sort of thing goes with the job and I'm tougher than I look. That's what you were thinking as we drove here, wasn't it?'

'What?'

'That I'm not sturdy enough for these sort of occasions,' she said teasingly.

'Yes. As a matter of fact, I *was* thinking that,' he admitted without an answering smile. 'Whatever possessed you to become a paramedic?'

'For the same reason as you, I would imagine. Because it's what I've always wanted to do. And don't get any wrong ideas. I love the job…just as you do.'

He managed a smile.

'That's me put in my place.'

Now it was her turn to be serious. 'No. Of course not.' With a catch in her voice, she added, 'It's nice to have someone concerned about me.'

And because he could no more not have asked it than flown to the moon, Kane questioned, 'What about that relative of your husband's? Doesn't he look out for you?'

'Peter?'

'Yes, I believe that's his name,' he said stiffly.

'Well, of course he does. He's family,' she said immediately.

But before she could explain that was all he was— Dave's family, not hers and never would be—the triage nurse called her over to assess how urgent her requirements were and Kane was left to his thoughts.

An X-ray showed that though there was much bruising Selina hadn't suffered any damage to her spine. As she walked stiffly back to the ambulance she said in fervent relief, 'Thank goodness for that. Any health problems on my part could be financially and physically disastrous.'

'Yes. I do realise that,' he said, still with an edge to his voice.

He was realizing something else as well. He was travelling on a road that he'd had no intentions of going along, and that he might have to turn back sharply if Selina ever found out about a certain nasty little incident in his past.

The sickening memory of Eve Richards's accusations had been pushed to the back of his mind, but he felt as if the taint of it would never leave him.

He'd always been popular with the opposite sex, never needed to chase a woman. But the Richards woman had made him sound like some sort of propositioning groper, and all because of her hurt pride.

As he brought his thoughts back to the moment Kane saw that Selina's gaze was on him, and with a swift change of subject he said, 'So where are we taking Josh and his two cousins over the weekend?'

Her face lit up and he thought whimsically that there was no guile in Selina.

'You haven't forgotten!'

'Of course I haven't. Did you think I would?'

'Er…well, no, not exactly.'

'And what is that supposed to mean?'

'I thought that you and Denise might—'

'What?'

'Be making arrangements.'

He almost laughed out loud. Denise was the last person he intended getting involved with. But he supposed that they had been spending a lot of time together when they were waiting to be called out at the ambulance station. It was one way of taking his mind off the woman seated beside him.

Denise had even suggested that they ask the station officer if she could ride with him instead of Selina, but he'd soon nipped that idea in the bud. Even if he hadn't been happy with Selina as a partner, Denise was the last person he would want to replace her. One oversexed female in his past was enough.

Just being with this young widow, who was observing him with violet eyes full of questions, seemed to be calming the turmoil past events had left inside him.

For the present he dared not think any further than that, and it might have been the reason why he didn't make it as clear as he could have done that Denise was of no interest to him.

Instead, he said casually, 'At the present time I'm not involved in making ''arrangements'', as you so delicately describe it, with Denise Hapgood. But I'll keep you informed.'

He saw a shadow cross her face and cursed himself for being a procrastinating fool. It wasn't in his nature to beat about the bush, but there was the garage fellow hovering in the background of Selina's life and the tender memories of her husband that were ever with her.

'You didn't answer my question about the children,' he reminded her.

Her expression lightened. 'No, I didn't, did I? How about a drive to the coast?'

'Mmm, sounds great. Blackpool maybe? The world-famous resort? I've always wanted to go there.'

Selina laughed.

'You might be disappointed. Kiss-me-quick hats, candy-floss and the tower.'

'That alone should be worth seeing. Let's go!'

'All right.' She sparkled. 'Blackpool it is.'

CHAPTER FIVE

'SO HOW'S the back?' were Kane's first words when he arrived to pick them up for the Blackpool trip.

Selina thought she saw anxiety in his glance and once again she was warmed by his concern. Yet perversely she brushed it to one side and said lightly, 'Much better, thanks.'

'Good,' he said impassively, as if aware that she was backing off. Turning his attention to Josh and the twins, he said, 'So, are we all ready to go to the seaside?'

'Yes!' the three young ones chorused.

Kane and Selina exchanged amused glances when Josh said, 'I don't want to sit in the back with those dolls. Can I be at the front with Kane?'

'All right,' Selina agreed. 'Men at the front and women in the back.'

The dolls he'd referred to were being held lovingly by Katie and Kirsty, and as they set off Selina thought that anyone seeing them would think they were a family out for the day—and how wrong they would be.

The little girls with the neat brown plaits belonged to Jill and Gavin. And Kane—who did he belong to? Nobody, she hoped. Or was there someone he was keeping under wraps? Yet he would hardly want to spend his day off with her and the three children if there was.

As the miles sped past along the M60 she could hear Josh chattering away to him and she wondered if her small son was remembering who had always been in the driving seat before.

But she was realistic enough to accept that children lived

for the day and if Josh was happy to have Kane there, so
was she. Very happy!

In fact, she felt as if she was coming alive again and it
was all because of the man in front of her. Her gaze was
on the tanned skin at the back of his neck beneath hair dark
as ravens' wings. Suddenly she wanted to touch him, to
feel the warm strength of him beneath her fingertips.

She clasped her hands tightly together in sudden panic,
as if afraid they might develop a will of their own, and for
the rest of the journey she looked steadfastly out of the
window.

They'd motored through Lytham with its lifeboat house and
huge windmill by the seashore, past the exclusively sedate
frontage of St Anne's-on-Sea, and now Blackpool, crowded
as always, was upon them.

The huge Pleasure Beach was looming up, with the metal
framework of the famous tower pointing heavenwards behind it. As the three children gazed around them, wide-
eyed, Selina said, 'What would you like to do the most?'

With their glances on the miles of golden sand stretching
as far as the eye could see, they chorused, 'The beach!'

'It's crowded,' Kane said doubtfully.

'Drive a few more miles along the promenade,' Selina
suggested. 'It will be quieter there.'

'Miles?' he questioned as dark brows rose. 'How long is
it?'

'Very,' she told him laughingly. 'It goes on for ever. It's
what makes this part of the Fylde Coast so popular. That
and the air, which is so bracing it blows all the cobwebs
away.'

Kane's smile was wry. It would take more than fresh air
to blow away the cobwebs in his life.

Soon he was going to start making plans. Was today
going to be the first step? he asked himself, only to have

the thought die at birth as Josh turned in his seat and said to his mother, 'I told Uncle Peter that we were going to the seaside and he said why hadn't we asked him to go with us.'

Kane watched Selina's colour rise and wondered why. Was she embarrassed because it sounded as if the other man wasn't pleased with her? He supposed it was possible that she and the mechanic did have some sort of an arrangement and she was feeling that maybe she'd overstepped the mark by spending the day with a comparative stranger.

Yet her reply was relaxed enough as she said to Josh, 'Maybe we'll ask him to come with us next time, eh?'

After the marriage proposal of the other night hell would have to freeze over before that happened, she was thinking, but Kane and Josh weren't to know that.

It was less crowded at the northern end of the resort and soon they were on the beach, complete with picnic basket, buckets and spades, a windbreak and a plentiful supply of towels.

As they settled into a spot that was reasonably quiet, Kane eyed the outgoing tide.

'The sea's pretty rough for such a flat shoreline,' he remarked. 'Do people get into difficulties here?'

Selina's expression was grave.

'Yes, sometimes. Mostly when the tide's right in and on the turn. Reckless youngsters start trying to dodge the waves. Or there have been occasions when someone has gone in after a dog that they were concerned about and have lost their own life.'

'And no doubt the dog calmly swam to safety.'

'Something like that. But don't let's talk about such things today,' she protested wistfully. 'I want to be happy and carefree!'

And fitting the action to the words, she slipped out of

the loose sundress she'd been travelling in to reveal a black one-piece bathing suit.

With arms uplifted she raised her face to the sun and the man watching felt desire rise in him. But the moment was brief. The children were clamouring to have their shoes off and bathing suits on, and he smiled.

Selina was safe. She had her own contingent of small guardian angels with her, and he didn't know whether to be glad or sorry.

They splashed about at the edge of the sea with the adults keeping a careful watch on their young charges. Made sand pies and decorated them with bright paper flags. Tucked into chicken nuggets, sandwiches, crisps and suchlike, and with the never-ending thirst of the young had drunk all the squash she'd packed.

And now, overcome by the sun and sea air, Katie and Kirsty had fallen asleep on one of the big beach towels.

Josh eyed them scornfully and started to make a sand castle, digging with a determination that was meant to show that he wasn't tired.

During the brief respite Kane went to swim in the sea, and as Selina watched him walk towards the water in a pair of brief bathing shorts her heartbeat quickened.

He was attracting attention from both sexes as he strode along, but she could tell by his measured stride and the way he looked to neither right nor left that he was either unaware of the fact or just wasn't interested.

As he entered the water she lay back, closed her eyes and tried to imagine what it would be like to make love with him. She'd moved on now. Her life with Dave had been good, but it was in the past. Nothing could bring him back. She was aware of the appeal of another man. So aware that she couldn't stop thinking about him.

Kane had erupted into her life on that dreadful day when

Josh had been knocked down outside school by a car, and ever since it had felt as if he belonged there.

Although perhaps 'erupted' wasn't quite the right word. There had been nothing volcanic about him so far. He was cool and contained and, though he knew all about her affairs, she knew little about his.

Maybe some time today she might get the chance to ask him about his family and his life before joining the city's paramedics, she thought drowsily.

As her thoughts drifted she wasn't aware that there was silence all around her until Kane's voice cried urgently from above, 'Selina! Where's Josh?'

She was upright in a second, gazing wildly around her. The sand castle was there, only half-made, but of Josh there was no sign.

'He was here a minute ago,' she faltered. 'Where can he have gone?'

The girls were still sleeping and he said, 'Stay here with Katie and Kirsty and I'll go and look for him. There are some sand dunes up near the road there. He might be playing amongst them.'

Without further comment he went striding off, droplets of salt water glistening on his back.

While he was gone Selina stopped everyone who came by and asked them frantically if they'd seen a small, fair-haired boy in red swimming shorts.

When every time the answer was no her panic increased and when Kane returned, grim-faced, with the news that he was nowhere to be seen, terror had her in its grip.

'Where can he be?' she cried tearfully. 'Josh was there, making the sand castle, when I closed my eyes. He can't have gone far, Kane.' Her voice croaking with dread. 'Unless he ventured after you into the sea while I had my eyes closed, and the current...'

Her voice trailed away at the thought of something too

horrible to contemplate. But an even worse thought had come into her mind and she had to voice it.

'Or somebody's taken him. Suppose somebody's taken him, Kane!'

He had produced a mobile phone out of the pocket of his shorts.

'I'm going to ring the police,' he said grimly. 'We're not taking any chances. When something like this happens time is of the essence.'

At that moment a line of donkeys appeared on the horizon, with two teenage boys in charge, and he said thankfully, 'Look, Selina! On the first donkey. He's been for a ride.'

'Oh! Thank goodness!' she breathed and promptly burst into tears.

'Come here,' he said softly. Holding her close, he gently stroked her hair.

'I couldn't bear it if anything happened to Josh,' she sobbed. 'He's all I've got. Love brings pain with it, Kane. Too much pain. I can't believe that he just took it into his head to wander off like that.'

'Here he comes,' he told her. 'Let's see what he has to say.'

An excited Josh was running towards them, full of the thrill of the donkey ride, and Selina said weakly, 'Josh, you had no right to go off without asking permission. Don't ever do that again! Where did you get the money from?'

His face crumpled.

'I used the money that Uncle Gavin gave me yesterday...and I did ask you. You had your eyes closed but I thought you'd heard me. You sort of nodded your head.'

'I don't remember any of that,' she said flatly, but she thought guiltily that she'd been miles away, daydreaming about Kane.

At that moment the twins woke up and wanted their turn

on the donkeys, but this time Selina, Kane and a subdued Josh were alongside them.

A last paddle and then it was time for home. Selina wasn't sorry. Those terrifying moments when she'd thought she'd lost Josh had left her with a headache and nausea...and regret as well, because she'd been too het up to appreciate being held in Kane's arms.

On the way back the children had chattered all the time, but Kane and Selina were silent, each of them deep in thought.

She couldn't be angry at Josh for long, but his wandering off had spoiled the day and she was wondering what Kane's thoughts were on the matter. Was he thinking that there were better ways to spend his time than with a panicking mother and a disobedient child?

When they'd dropped the twins off she said hesitantly, 'Would you like to come in and have something to eat with us, Kane? It won't be anything special but you're very welcome.'

She found that she was holding her breath, yet it wouldn't be the end of the world if he said no, would it? He might have something planned for later.

He smiled for the first time since they'd left the coast. She looked tired and windblown and was recovering from a nasty shock. He couldn't let her cook for him.

'Yes, I'd like to eat with you both, but only as long as you agree to me going to get us a take-away.'

'Mmm, that would be great,' she said, her spirits rising now that he didn't want to rush off home. 'And while you're gone I'm going to wash the salt out of my hair, and this young man can have a bath and then get into his pyjamas.'

Was Selina telling him something? Kane wondered as he drove off. That shortly after they'd eaten they would be alone? Somehow he didn't think it was likely.

In her frantic concern over Josh she'd told him that love hurt. As if its pain outweighed its joy. He supposed she had cause to feel like that. She'd suffered a great loss and now, because of it, had a horror of anything happening to her son.

Yet the fact remained that she'd cast a spell over him. It was as if he'd been waiting for her all his life, and now that she was there, what was he going to do about it?

Tell her, of course. The moment they were alone he would tell Selina how he felt and take his chances.

There was the garage looming up in front of him again and 'Uncle Peter' on the forecourt. The fellow was haunting him, and if the baleful glare that was coming his way was anything to go by, it would seem that the feeling was mutual.

Too bad, buddy, he thought as he drove past. We might both be playing a losing game, but I'm all set for a try.

When he got back they were waiting for him, Josh scrubbed and clean in his pyjamas and Selina with the fair swathe of her hair lying damply against her head.

They were smiling their welcome and Kane felt his chest tighten. His recollections of family life were so far back they were almost non-existent.

There had been a house full of them, noisy, rumbustious, but a family nevertheless. Until his father had walked out and left them penniless. His mother hadn't been able to cope and had put half of them into care. He'd been one of them.

Surprisingly, they'd lived under better conditions than before, but the closeness hadn't been there and once he'd reached manhood he'd gone his own way.

'So,' he said lightly as Selina fetched the plates that had been warming, 'let's eat.'

By the time Josh was in bed a summer dusk was throwing shadows across the room and Selina got up to switch on the lamps. She'd been longing to be alone with Kane, but now the moment had arrived she was nervous. Was she imagining that there was chemistry between them?

He'd told her when they'd first met that he preferred to be the hunter rather than the hunted. Was he thinking that she'd got him labelled as husband material?

Instead of going back to sit beside him on the couch, she sat down in the chair facing him and turned her head away from his dark intent gaze.

'What's wrong, Selina?' he asked. 'Do you want me to go?'

'No! I mean, yes! They don't like staff to cohabit in the ambulance service,' she gabbled in inane desperation.

That brought him to his feet and he stood looking down on her in amused amazement.

'Cohabit? With you at one side of the room and me on the other? We'd earn a place in the *Guinness Book of Records*.'

Tears were sparkling on her lashes.

'Don't laugh at me, Kane. No man has touched me since Dave died. I feel like a nervous virgin.'

He reached out and drew her slowly out of her chair.

'There's no need to be nervous, Selina, and I'm not laughing at you. You're young and beautiful and I've wanted to make love to you ever since we met, but—'

She put a finger to his lips.

'No buts. Just hold me, Kane.' As he enfolded her in his arms and kissed her with a passion that she'd never expected to experience again, it was there once more, the feeling of coming out of darkness.

How long they were locked in each other's arms she didn't know. It was enough to know that Kane found her desirable.

Easing herself gently out of his arms, she took his hand and led him towards the stairs. Smiling up at him, she said,

'I can't believe that we've come so far so soon. Yet it feels so right, even though I know nothing about you. My past and present are an open book to you, but yours aren't to me. Tell me about yourself, Kane. Where you come from. About your family and friends. What makes you tick. I want to know everything about you.

'Charlie came round the other night and I had the feeling that he was warning me off you. That he knew something about you but was reluctant to tell me. I fobbed him off by telling him that to me you are merely someone I work with…which was untrue.'

Kane's face had whitened. They were standing with their arms around each other at the bottom of the stairs and he stifled a groan. Of all times, Selina had chosen this moment to ask questions.

There was no way he was going to lie to her. It wasn't his style. Letting his arms fall away from her, he said tonelessly, 'So you want to know all about me. Then I'd better tell you. I'm one of a family of eight. My father left us when I was quite small, and as my mother was almost penniless she put some of us into care. I was one of them.'

'Oh, no!' she breathed.

'Oh, yes, I'm afraid. When I was old enough to fend for myself I did just that and nothing has changed. Since those early days I've never been really close to anyone…until now. I've had relationships but none of them mattered. Maybe that's what got to Eve Richards so much.'

'And who might she be?' Selina asked slowly.

'She was my partner on the ambulance before I moved up here. Eve developed a grand passion for me and it got out of hand. When I decided to change jobs to get away from her, she accused me of sexual harassment.'

Selina felt her jaw go slack.

'So you were having an affair with her…and then decided you'd had enough?' she questioned dismally.

The enchantment of those moments in his arms was slipping away. She'd asked for it, but did she want to hear this?

'It wasn't like that. I wasn't having an affair with her. She didn't appeal to me one bit,' he said in grim denial.

For the first time ever he was ready to tell someone of the misery and embarrassment he'd suffered, and who better than Selina with her uncomplicated generosity of spirit? But as he braced himself to speak she forestalled him.

'It all sounds very unpleasant. You wouldn't have told me if I hadn't insisted, would you?' she said flatly. 'You would have let us go on from where we were a few moments ago and I would have been none the wiser.'

Frustration was rising in him.

'Correct, and from where I'm standing it seems that would have been the best thing to do. Look at you! You're acting as if I'm guilty of what I was accused of. For your information I was completely exonerated. It was discovered that she had mental problems.

'But why am I telling you this? What happened is my affair and no one else's, and if you're peeved because I was intending to make love to you without having ''confessed'', it's because I have nothing to hide.'

'I see. So there was no truth in the allegation.'

He raked his dark locks with a restless hand.

'I can't believe you asked me that. But I suppose it's only reasonable. As you said before, you hardly know me and you wouldn't want Josh—or yourself for that matter— associating with an unsavoury character.'

He was lifting his jacket off the hallstand.

'I'm going, Selina. I think we've both said enough for one night.'

'No!' she protested. 'Don't let us part like this, Kane.'

'Look, Selina, you have only my word for it that I was innocent. You'll have to decide whether you believe me or not. All I know is that I'm still paying for something I didn't do. What has just happened between us is proof of that.' And without giving her the chance to persuade him further, he opened the door and went.

As Selina went slowly upstairs she felt numb. The last thing she'd expected when she'd asked Kane to tell her about himself had been that it would cause a rift between them. And now he had gone, hurt and angry.

But what about her? What had he expected her to say when she discovered that it was only her persistence that had made him tell her about Eve Richards?

He'd left thinking that she'd judged him unfairly when all she'd wanted had been for them to talk it through. That it was a sore topic had been very plain to see. So where did they go from here? Not very far, she thought dismally.

She had to talk to him again, she thought wretchedly as she eyed the bedside phone, but how? She had neither a phone number nor an address.

The only thing she knew was that he lived in an apartment in a high-rise block not far from where they worked. Which showed how little she knew about him. She had been right to insist he tell her something about himself, she thought bleakly. Did Kane think she was in the habit of making love with strangers?

But her expression softened as she remembered that there were things that she did know about him. She knew that he was the best paramedic she'd ever seen in action and that, though he could be reticent at times, he was thoughtful and quick to understand. He didn't push himself where Josh was concerned, and until last night had never laid a finger on her, except for that fleeting moment one afternoon when he'd held her hand in the ambulance.

There's no smoke without fire, the voice of reason said. If you want to know more there is someone you can ring—

Charlie Vaughan. He should have told you what was in his mind the other night, instead of chickening out.

But even as she was picking up the phone she knew that she couldn't do it. Kane was hurting enough without her making things worse by turning to tittle-tattle.

The next day Selina wandered around the cottage, restless and on edge, praying that the phone might ring and it would be Kane telling her that he understood the way she'd reacted and could they start afresh? But it remained frustratingly silent.

At last she was back on the job and she'd never been more eager to be there.

The moment they were alone in the ambulance she was going to talk to Kane. Tell him that what he'd told her had been a shock, but now that she'd adjusted, couldn't they at least be friends?

Once that was done she would take it one step at a time and hope that she could take away his hurt and anger. She wasn't such a poor judge of character that she would fall in love with a man of questionable morals.

Their first call of the day was to a suspected heart attack, and as the ambulance swung beneath the huge metal doors and out onto the nearby motorway, Selina was ready to say her piece.

In her eagerness to see him again she'd been the first of the day shift to arrive, but unfortunately Kane had been the last and until the call had come through he hadn't even looked in her direction.

But now there was no getting away from each other. They were a team. Whatever was going on in the background of their lives, this was what they were employed to do and, as if to remind her of that fact, he forestalled anything she might have been about to say by telling her abruptly, 'I'm only prepared to talk about the job, Selina, and if you want to ask permission to change partners, it's all right with me.'

She knew that she had to stay calm.

'I see you're determined to get the first word in. Is it all right if I say something now?' she asked as they turned onto the road where the call had come from.

'Yes. As long as you do as you're told,' he replied, the chill persisting.

'Right. First of all I don't want to work with anyone else but you. So I'm not going to ask for the arrangement to be changed. Yes?'

He still had the shuttered look about him. 'So, you're prepared to take the risk.'

'If there is one…yes.'

She was denied the chance to say anything else because Kane was stopping the ambulance in front of a neat detached house. As they pushed open the front door a voice called from above. 'We're up here!'

He went up the narrow staircase two steps at a time and Selina was close behind. They both knew that if it was a heart attack these first minutes were vital.

In a bedroom at the front of the house an elderly man in dressing-gown and pyjamas was lying on the floor with an anxious woman of a similar age bending over him. He was fighting for breath and clutching at his chest. His eyes were closed, his skin was clammy, and as Kane delved into the advance response bag Selina quickly unfastened his clothing to bare his chest.

'Is it his heart?' the woman asked shakily. 'He'd just brought me a cup of tea up and down he went. He's been in too much pain for me to move him so I just put a pillow under his head.'

She was ashen with shock and Selina gave her a reassuring smile.

'We need to get your husband to hospital as quickly as

possible so how about packing a bag while we're treating him?'

'Er…yes. I'll do that,' she faltered, eager to be of use.

'We'll do an ECG first,' Kane said quickly. 'If the heart muscles are in the state I think they are, we'd better be ready to defibrillate.'

The ECG showed that there was ventricular fibrillation present, and as they worked on the patient together Selina thought that, whatever was going on in the background of their lives, this was where they were in tune.

They had a very sick patient who might die before they got him to hospital, but not if they could help it. They would fight to save him every inch of the way, and once they'd done their part the coronary unit would take over.

The heart rhythm improved with the electric shock treatment and the pain killers they gave him were reducing the agony inside his chest so there would be some slight improvement when they handed him over to the trauma team. But during the next few hours the man's life would be in grave danger, in spite of the prompt attention he'd received.

'They want us to station ourselves near the entrance to the university for the rest of the day,' Kane said after they'd delivered the man to A and E. 'It seems that it's another accident black spot.'

Selina's thoughts were on the tearful woman they'd just left. She had a long vigil ahead of her. Selina had got her a cup of tea and phoned the woman's daughter to ask her to join her mother. It wasn't much, but it was better than nothing.

'We're not supposed to get personal on this job, Selina,' Kane reminded her in a milder tone than the one he'd used before.

She took her gaze off the road in front and observed him

with troubled eyes. 'Are you talking about my concern for the people we meet or you and I, Kane?'

'Both.'

'I see. Well, with regard to us, you're going to have to hear me out whether you like it or not. First of all I want to apologise for the way I behaved the other night. For one thing you were a guest in my house and I should have kept my opinions to myself.'

She sighed. 'It all started because I wanted to know more about you and I got more than I bargained for, but it occurred to me after you'd gone that I still don't know your address or phone number.'

He shrugged and she knew by the way of it that there wasn't going to be a quick resolution of their misunderstanding.

'Does it matter?' he said stiffly.

'Yes, it does to me. I've spent the last thirty-six hours desperate to talk to you, but didn't know how to get in touch.'

When there was no reply forthcoming she said, 'I'm going to get something to eat at the shop over there. Can I get you anything?'

He shook his head and so, swinging long legs out of the driving seat, she straightened up and made her way to a nearby sandwich shop.

She wasn't really hungry. She hadn't felt like eating since the distressing events of the other night, but it was a relief to be away from Kane for a few moments.

If they went on like this she wouldn't be able to bear it. Being cooped up together with all the lovely rapport gone. She might even end up doing what he'd suggested. Asking to be put with someone else.

Why was he so prickly, she wondered, if there was nothing in what he'd told her? Lots of men might feel it was

macho to be described in such a manner. But not Kane
Kavener, it would seem.

The fact remains that in your case a little knowledge
turned out to be a dangerous thing, she told herself. And if
you're going to continue yearning for him under those circumstances, you're a fool, Selina Sanderson.

CHAPTER SIX

YOU'RE behaving like an idiot, Kane told himself as Selina climbed back on board with a packet of drab-looking sandwiches. His enchanting partner was trying to understand and he was being deliberately difficult.

But he had his pride, for heaven's sake! The injustice that Eve Richards had done him was still blighting his life and he was damned if he was going to start protesting his innocence to a fresh lot of people.

He didn't now what Charlie Vaughan had heard, but as in all big organisations there was a grapevine that had far-spreading branches. Whatever it was, it had brought about a confrontation between Selina and himself that had left her dumbstruck and dismayed.

Selina, who had other men in her life. Men who'd known her much longer than he had, and wouldn't allow anyone to harm her.

There was the hovering cousin, her brother and, to the forefront in recent days, Charlie Vaughan. They were her protectors and it would be easier to break into Fort Knox than get past the 'keep your hands off Selina' vigilantes if he put a foot wrong.

The last thing he would ever want would be to cause her distress and, with angry frustration still churning inside him, it seemed as if the best way to avoid hurting her was to stand back. Keep a hold on his emotions and let the job be their only contact.

He wasn't the only one coming to conclusions. As she munched on the unappetising food Selina was making a painful decision of her own and he was about to be told what it was.

'Until you feel that you can talk to me I don't see any future for us, Kane. You're not even giving me the chance to understand what this is all about,' she said wearily. 'I suppose I should ask to be moved, but as I've done nothing wrong I don't see why I should. So in the meantime I suggest we get on with what we're paid for while you keep your secrets and I keep my peace of mind.'

'My feelings exactly,' he said abruptly. 'What you don't know about, you won't fret about.'

That will be the day, she thought miserably. She was in love with him for better or worse. But he was stubborn, secretive and totally insensitive to treat her like this.

'Love hurts,' she'd told him that day on Blackpool beach when Josh had been missing, and it seemed as if nothing had changed.

A green call was coming through to attend a pedestrian with a suspected fracture from a fall, and once again they had to put their own affairs on hold.

'Why doesn't Kane come to see us any more?' Josh asked on the night before they were off to visit her father-in-law in Devon.

'Maybe he's busy,' she said evasively.

Josh frowned.

'Too busy to come and see us?'

'I think he might be house-hunting. He lives in a flat and doesn't like it very much.'

'He could come and live with us. He told me that he likes it round here.'

'Did he? When was that?'

'The day we went to the seaside.'

'Hmm. I see.'

It was ironic, she thought later as she sat alone in front

of the television. Lots of women in her position had problems with their children when they tried to introduce the new man in their lives. Yet in her case it hadn't been like that. Josh had taken to Kane right from the start. But sadly there had been other problems to blight their relationship.

She didn't really want to go away but she couldn't deny her father-in-law the chance to spend some time with his grandson, and in a way it would be a relief to get away from the ambulance station for a while.

Kane would be working with Denise while she was gone. The other woman hadn't hesitated when Mark had suggested it and Selina had thought miserably that he might cheer up with the uncomplicated redhead as his partner. Although, in the light of recent events, she'd have thought he'd have asked for one of the men to assist him.

Since their separate ultimatums they had adopted a polite sort of truce and if she went home each night feeling lost and miserable, at least she knew where she stood.

Josh woke up in the early hours with a high temperature, and when Selina examined him she saw that there were small watery blisters behind his ears and on his body.

'Oh, dear,' she said. 'It looks as if Grandad is in for a disappointment. I think you've got chickenpox.'

'You mean we can't go to Devon?'

'I'm afraid not. Chickenpox isn't a very serious illness in children, but if an older person picks up the virus it becomes shingles and that can be very unpleasant. We'll have to ring him first thing in the morning to tell him what's happened.'

She placed her hand on his hot little brow.

'And what about you? Are you very disappointed?'

'Yes. But we can go another time, can't we?'

'Of course. But we might have to wait until I have some more holidays due.'

She went downstairs to get him a drink and some paracetamol and within minutes he was asleep again. As she
stood looking down on him, Selina reminded herself to
check the medicine cabinet for calamine lotion in prepa-
ration for when the blisters became dry and scratchy.

When she went back to her own bed she lay, wide-eyed,
thinking about the latest turn of events. Robert would be
very upset that they weren't going, but he would be a lot
more distraught if he caught shingles.

As for herself, she was sorry to let him down but relieved
at the same time. He was a shrewd old guy and if he picked
up on the fact that she had something on her mind, he
wouldn't rest until he knew what it was—and what would
he think when he found out that there was another man in
her life?

But also, and far more important, she wasn't going to be
miles away from Kane, even though her affairs seemed to
be of no interest to him any more.

Her father-in-law's reaction to the news next morning
was as she'd expected—disappointed, followed by a reluctant consideration for his own health that helped him to
accept that the visit was off.

As he put the phone down Selina breathed a sigh of
relief. It was a disappointment for Josh and his granddad,
but the up side of it was that she was already on leave so
she would be there during the next two weeks while the
chickenpox took its course.

They would have to stay away from Gavin and his family
in the hope that it wouldn't be passed on to Katie and
Kirsty. But she knew there was a strong possibility that it
already had been, as chicken pox is most contagious before
the blisters appear.

In the middle of that first week they went for an early
morning walk along the canalside so that Josh could see
the boats moored at the marina.

It was a warm, clear day and as he skipped along in front of her Selina was thankful that the chickenpox hadn't made him feel ill. He was still spotty but they were drying off and liberal applications of the calamine were helping to stop him from scratching.

As she walked along behind him, her mind was elsewhere. What would Kane be doing at this moment? she wondered. Speeding across the city to answer a call? Or tucked up inside the close confines of the ambulance with the sexy Denise? She wished she knew. But what did it matter any more? She'd had a brief glimpse of happiness and then what? Nothing.

It was quiet when they reached the marina. Those who lived on the water weren't yet up and about and the visitors hadn't so far put in an appearance.

There was a new boat there that hadn't been at the moorings the last time they'd gone past, and they stopped to admire its gleaming paintwork and shiny brass fittings.

'Can we go inside and have a look?' Josh asked, wide-eyed at its splendour.

She smiled.

'No, not really. The owners might be asleep down below and in any case it would be trespassing.'

'Aw, Mum,' he wheedled. 'They wouldn't know if we were very quiet.'

'No, Josh,' she was repeating firmly when the figure of a man came into view, striding briskly along the towpath. He was carrying a bottle of milk and a loaf of bread and he nearly dropped them when he saw the two of them standing by the boat.

If he was surprised, Selina was dumbstruck. Only Josh saw nothing unusual in the occasion.

'Kane!' he cried as he ran towards him. 'Is it your boat?'

'Yes,' he said. Putting down the groceries, he held out his arms and swung Josh high in the air.

Selina hadn't moved. What was going on? Kane living only a few minutes' walk from them! That was all she needed. It was bad enough coping with his nearness on the job, but this was unbelievable.

'Hello, Selina,' he said when they drew level, 'I thought that you were going to Devon.'

'Obviously,' she said coolly. 'We had to cancel the holiday because Josh has got chickenpox. How long have you been living here?'

'Hmm, good thing I've been vaccinated!' He shot her a smile, which quickly faded as he saw that the coolness had reached her eyes. 'I moved in over the weekend.'

'I see. Choosing a time when I wouldn't be around? And as usual keeping your affairs strictly to yourself.'

'If that's how you want to see it, yes.'

'Can we go on the boat?' Josh asked.

Kane hesitated and at that moment a voice Selina recognised called from down below in the cabin, 'Kane, who's that you're talking to? I need paracetamol. I've got a splitting headache.'

He leaned over the rail and called down uncomfortably, 'Hold on. I'll be with you in a moment.' He turned to Josh, who was waiting for an answer. 'Maybe later on, Josh. This afternoon perhaps...if that's all right with your mother.'

'Yes,' she told him stiffly. 'Just as long as you don't expect me to come with him.'

His face was expressionless.

'So you're going to trust me with him, even though I'm seen as an unsavoury character?'

'I've never said that, Kane,' she said in the same tight tone. Taking Josh's hand firmly in hers, she moved off.

He had some nerve, that one, she thought furiously as

they walked back home. Moving into the village when he thought her back was turned…and with this girlfriend.

Where had it all gone? she thought dismally. The magic of getting to know each other? The tenderness that had helped start the healing process after long months of grief and loneliness?

'Selina! Here a minute.'

It was Peter, calling across from the garage.

'Yes. What is it?' she asked warily.

'I thought you guys were going to Grandad Sanderson's?'

'We were, but Josh has got chickenpox and we didn't want to start a shingles epidemic in Devon.'

'I see. I see something else as well. That your boyfriend has got a barge on the marina.'

'It didn't take you long to find that out.'

'I hear all the village gossip in this place.'

'So it would seem.'

'The romance is still on, then?'

'Yes. It's going great guns,' she fibbed sweetly, 'and now, if you'll excuse us, we have an appointment with a bottle of calamine lotion.'

If she'd been fed up before, the conversation with Peter had increased it tenfold. Why couldn't they all leave her to get on with her own life? Selina though as she brought the washing in and began to iron it.

The boat Kane had bought was beautiful and she supposed that he was entitled to do as he chose, but how was she going to sleep on warm autumn nights, knowing that he was so near yet so far away?

Typical of him, he'd bought somewhere to live that had no permanency with it. He could sail to another mooring whenever he chose. So maybe his appearance at the marina hadn't anything to do with her.

And as for the thing he wouldn't talk about, it hadn't sounded as if Denise was complaining of any sexual harassment.

Kane came for Josh at two o'clock in the afternoon and when Selina stood back to let him in he shook his head.

'I'd rather not if you don't mind. I have unpleasant memories of the last time I was here.'

Selina glared at him.

'Mine aren't too rosy either.'

He shrugged his shoulders and that did it. She wanted to shake him and lunged at him angrily, but before she could touch him he had gripped her wrists.

'They say there's only a fine line between hate and love,' he told her quietly, 'and it looks as if you've crossed it, Selina. Maybe I ought to bring you back.'

'What do you mean?' she breathed as his grasp tightened.

'This,' he said softly. 'And if any of your protectors are watching they can make of it what they will.'

He released his grip on her wrists and, taking her face between his hands, kissed her with a passionate thoroughness that made her weak with longing.

When he'd finished she sank back against the doorpost. As if on cue, Josh came running round the side of the house and cried, 'Hi, Kane. I'm ready.'

'Good,' he said calmly. 'We'll be off, then. Can he stay for dinner?'

Selina was rallying. 'Only if you haven't got company,' she said with cool sarcasm.

'I haven't. I could give you an explanation for what happened earlier, but I'm sure you won't want to hear it.'

'I don't,' she said abruptly, and with a quick kiss for Josh she finished, 'I'll see you both later.'

Then with what remained of her dignity she went in and closed the door. That done Selina put a hand to her lips.

They were still warm from Kane's mouth. What sort of game was he playing?

Kane would have realised how she'd sprung to life at his touch, yet she felt instinctively that he wasn't going to do anything further about it.

It was late evening when he brought Josh back and her son was sweatily ecstatic.

'We've been painting a name on the boat, Mum!' he cried as he came running up the path with Kane close behind.

'Really?' she exclaimed with a weak attempt at enthusiasm. 'That must have been great fun. What have you called it? *The Clam*? After its owner?'

Kane got the message and Selina saw his eyes glint, but Josh was too excited to decipher veiled comments.

'No. Nothing like that. We've called it *The Joshua*.'

'You have? My goodness!'

Her eyes were tender as she gazed down at him, but when she lifted her head there was disbelief in the look she directed at Kane.

'How could you do that?' she asked when Josh had gone to take off his soiled clothes. 'You've made it clear that what we had is over, due to your stupid pride, and now you've called the boat after Josh. He'll want to be round there all the time after this.'

'I'm not going to be there all that much, am I, with the kind of hours we work?' he said levelly. 'And when I am there he will be most welcome.'

'Why didn't you moor your boat somewhere else instead of on my doorstep?'

'I'm not sure what the answer to that is,' he said with the irritating calm that he displayed every time she was on edge. 'But I'm sure that one of your many protectors will be watching over you while the sex maniac is around.'

'And now I'm off, Selina. Even if *you're* on holiday, I'm not. I'm on nights for the next two shifts and then days. So you see, I won't be around all that much to annoy you.' And off he went.

As she watched him stride off in the direction of the marina she wanted to run after him and tell him that he didn't annoy her. That she was puzzled, hurt and head over heels in love with him. But the first move had to come from him. If he couldn't confide in her, knowing how much she cared, then there was nothing else to be said.

Walking back along the towpath, Kane was admitting to himself that Selina was right. He *had* gone behind her back with his purchase of the boat. And he *should* have moored it somewhere else.

But the only reason he'd bought it had been to be near her, in spite of his protestations to the contrary. He still desperately wanted Lock-Keeper's Cottage, but he'd shelved that idea. If he wasn't going to be living in it with Selina and Josh, there was no point in making an offer for it.

Why couldn't he sink his pride? Go back and pour out his hurts and miseries to her as he'd been about to do on the night that they'd quarrelled? But she had enough of her own without having to listen to his, and he still didn't know what she really thought about the things he'd told her.

Then there was the catastrophe of Denise being on the boat when Selina and Josh had stopped by. That was something else he hadn't handled very well. He should have insisted on explaining. Should have told her that Denise had badgered him to take her to see his new home and eventually, because he'd had nothing better to do, he'd agreed, not expecting that she would bring enough wine with her to sink the *Titanic*, let alone *The Joshua*.

She'd been so drunk when it had been time for her to

leave that he'd had no choice but to let her sleep in the cabin for the night while he'd bedded down on the hard boards of the deck.

When he'd seen Selina and Josh beside the boat he'd felt that nothing worse could possibly happen, but it had.

While they'd been trying to decide on a name for it he'd let the pleading in the boy's eyes make him forget that he was supposed to be keeping a low profile with the Sanderson family, and the outcome of it had been *The Joshua*.

For someone who usually had a strong grip on life he was making a total mess of everything at the moment, and all because he didn't want to rake up the nightmare of Eve Richards's fabrications.

He was thrilled with the boat and the job was as rewarding as always, so why did he feel as if he was groping his way through fog?

By the time the fortnight was up Josh was almost clear of the chickenpox. Robert had phoned a couple of times and suggested that they now make the postponed visit but, as Selina had patiently explained, any other leave due to her would have to be saved for a break at Christmas and emergencies.

On her first morning back at work she had Kane's car in front of her most of the way through the early morning traffic, and thought soberly that this was how it was going to be, always under each other's feet when off duty.

Yet she'd seen nothing of him since the day he'd kissed her into limp submission and then left her to recover while he'd taken Josh back to the boat.

He had phoned a few times to ask if the boy wanted to go for a sail with him along the narrow waterway and Josh had jumped at the chance.

There had been no invitations for her, which had been

no surprise, and he'd picked Josh up at their front gate and dropped him off in the same place when the outings were over.

But today it would be different. Hopefully Denise would be back in her old slot and Kane and herself would be together once more on the job.

They arrived at the ambulance station at the same time, and as she locked her car Selina was aware of Kane doing the same thing only yards away.

'And so how are you today?' he enquired politely, as if they were distant acquaintances. 'Glad to be back?'

'Yes. I am, as a matter of fact.'

'Why would that be?'

Suddenly she'd had enough shilly-shallying.

'I love the job, for one thing. And for another I wanted to be with you again. You've gone out of your way to avoid me during the last two weeks.'

'Just a moment,' he interrupted. 'My boat is only five minutes' walk from your house. What was to prevent you from coming to find me?'

'I'm not the one who's created this situation,' she parried. 'But it looks as if I'm the only one who's bothered about sorting it out.'

Kane had the remote look about him that she was beginning to dread, but he did oblige with a comment of his own.

'Listen, Selina, one of the reasons I've been staying away from you is because I don't want any of the mud that's on me to rub off on you.'

'I might go along with that,' she flung back at him, 'if I knew where it had come from.'

'I resigned from my last job because the woman I worked with accused me of sexual harassment.'

'We've had a similar conversation before,' she said wearily. 'This is the moment where I ask you if it was true.'

'Of course it damn well wasn't! But no one was prepared to believe me until…'

'Until what?'

His glance had shifted to a silver Corsair pulling up beside them, but Selina wouldn't have cared if it had been a moon buggy. She was desperate to know and he was about to tell her.

'Hello, there,' Denise said as she swung her legs out of the car. 'I see that everybody's dream girl is back.'

Selina ignored the sarcastic comment and, looking Kane in the eye, said in a low voice, 'You were saying?'

'Forget it, Selina,' he replied. 'Let's just leave things as they are.' And with a tight smile that included Denise, who was hovering like a curious bird of prey, he concluded, 'Let's go and do what we're here for, shall we?'

Doing what they were there for included a first call-out to a man found in a coma in the local park.

'It looks like hypoglycaemia,' Kane said, 'but we'll need to check the blood-sugar level first. Let's get him on board.'

When they used the blood-sugar test kit on the unconscious man it confirmed that there was diabetes present and they gave him an immediate injection of glucagon to bring the sugar level back to normal.

'How long would you expect it to be before it takes effect?' Kane asked as they headed for the nearest A and E department.

'Fifteen to twenty minutes,' she answered promptly.

He nodded approvingly.

'Go to the top of the class. You *are* going to take your paramedics exams, I hope?'

'Yes. I am,' Selina said firmly. 'Lots of the trainees don't bother to go any further as the difference in pay is so small.'

'But you don't see it like that?'

'No. If a person is really dedicated they'll want to be a paramedic. It's as simple as that.'

'Everything is always clear cut where you're concerned, isn't it, Selina?' he said wryly. 'Black or white. No greys.'

'I suppose it is,' she agreed, 'and not so long ago it was all black…until you came along.'

He glanced quickly over his shoulder from the driving seat.

'And what is it now?'

'Black once more…because you've shut me out.'

She was monitoring the patient carefully and at that moment his eyelids lifted slightly.

'He's coming round, Kane,' she said.

'Good. We'll be there in a matter of seconds and then the emergency guys can take over. Will your brother be on duty this morning?'

'I'm not sure. He might be. Gavin and Jill have got their hands full at the moment. Both the girls have got chickenpox and, unlike Josh, they're quite poorly with it.'

His face softened.

'Poor little things.'

She cast a quick sideways glance at the face that haunted her dreams.

'You love children, don't you?'

'Mmm. I suppose I do.'

'Wouldn't you like some of your own?'

'Some day, maybe.'

Yes, she thought, and if we carry on the way we're doing, it won't be with me.

Another message was coming up on the computer screen. 'Entrapment in the city centre opposite Woolworths,' it said. 'Two teenagers trapped in car. Elderly pedestrian underneath the vehicle. Fast-response person at scene requests ambulance.'

'We're about to deliver a patient in a diabetic coma to

A and E,' Kane told control when he radioed in. 'As soon as we've handed him over we'll be on our way.'

'Fine,' was the reply. 'You're the nearest.'

They eyed the scene sombrely as Kane stopped the ambulance a few minutes later outside the department store. They were all there—police, firefighters and John Everett, the fast-response paramedic who had been on the scene from the ambulance services.

A forty-five-year-old with a jaundiced view on life since his wife had left him, he was efficient and kept calm under stress. But Selina didn't like him all that much as he'd been one of those who'd thought that because she was a widow she would be an easy catch.

His clumsy attempt at seduction had made her very wary of him, but that was the last thing on her mind as she looked around her.

One of the teenage boys had been freed from the wreckage of the car by the firemen, and John was bending over him while the other lad was being slowly eased out.

From the man half under the car there was an ominous silence, and as they took in the situation the fire chief said, 'We can't lift the car until the other lad is free, then it will be all systems go.'

Leaving him to his problems, Kane and Selina hurried to theirs.

'Massive head and chest injuries,' John said. 'He'd swallowed his tongue, but I was just in time to deal with it. You're going to have to get him to hospital faster than fast. I hope there're more ambulances on the way.'

'Yes, there are,' Selina told him. 'We were the nearest.'

Within moments they were stretchering the first casualty into the ambulance, and as they carefully laid him on the bed Kane said, 'He's arrested, Selina! No pulse. No heartbeat. We're going to have to jump-start him!'

She was at his side with the equipment before the words

had left his mouth. There'd been accident victims before who'd died before they could get them to hospital, and she accepted it happened sometimes. They couldn't work miracles, but when it was a young person in a life-threatening state it was like a knife turning inside her.

The youth was breathing again and as they looked at each other triumphantly. Kane's glance was warm. He'd felt her anguish and with the incredible tenderness that she aroused in him he'd wanted the lad to come back to life, if only for Selina's sake.

While they'd been treating him two more ambulances had arrived and the other teenager was being carried into one of them, while the third vehicle was waiting to take on board the body of the pedestrian who had died in the accident.

'What do you think happened?' Selina said as they drove to the hospital with sirens blaring.

'Possibly a stolen car that they couldn't control and the old guy stepped out in front of them. After they'd hit him they swerved into the bollards and then ran into the low wall around the store.'

She sighed. 'Youthful stupidity. Will they never learn? Much as I love the job, I wish something good could happen once in a while. It's all the down side of life, isn't it?'

'I've told you before, Selina, you're too gentle for this job…too soft-hearted to be involved in the kind of things we have to deal with.'

'Rubbish!' she scoffed laughingly. 'I'm tougher than you think. Is that why you're so anxious to keep your past under wraps? Because you think I'd be horrified if I knew what you'd been up to?'

He didn't join in the laughter. 'I haven't been up to anything.'

She was serious now and snappy with it. 'Then why all the ridiculous secrecy?'

'Ever since my teens I've been answerable to nobody,' he told her bleakly. 'That's what it does to you when you've been part of a large family where there's no privacy, no feeling of identity. And from there, as I've already explained, I was catapulted into care, where there was even less opportunity to be one's own person. So, you see, Selina, I treasure my privacy and when someone butts into it I back off.'

She was observing him with hurt eyes.

'So I'm butting in, am I? That's how you see me in your life. As an inquisitive hanger-on?'

Kane groaned softly. He'd been referring to Eve Richards's obsessive behaviour and consequent falsehoods. Selina could 'butt' into his life as much as she liked, if only he wasn't seen by some as tarnished goods.

Before he could explain, another urgent message came through to go to 34 Bentinck Street where a woman was in advanced labour.

Selina's expression lightened. Thank goodness, this time it wasn't anyone hurt and suffering. Just a member of her own sex doing what came naturally.

CHAPTER SEVEN

THE woman who opened the door to them was gasping with pain. At a glance they could both see that the baby was very low, and as she was gripped by another contraction almost immediately it was clear that there was no time to be lost.

'How long is it since your waters broke?' Selina asked as she swayed in front of them into a back sitting room.

'A couple of hours ago. I've been hanging on, hoping I could get in touch with my husband before I called you, but I can't contact him and as I had a fast labour with my first child I thought I'd better not wait any longer.'

'Good thinking,' Kane said briskly. 'Have you got a bag packed?'

She nodded.

'Right. Let's be off, then.'

As Selina helped her carefully into the ambulance, he said in a low voice. 'Have you ever delivered a baby?'

'Er...no. Have you?'

'Yes. A couple of times. It's an experience one doesn't forget.'

'I'll bet,' she agreed with an anxious glance at the mother-to-be.

When the expectant mother had been helped onto the bed Kane said, 'I'll drive, Selina. The lady will feel more comfortable with you in attendance.'

She could barely hear him as another of the frequent contractions was starting and this time the woman was screaming out loud.

'Keep doing the breathing exercises you've been prac-

108

tising,' Selina told her gently, 'and try to keep calm. You're going to be just fine. I'm going to see how far you are.' As the woman began to cry out again while Selina was examining her, she took her hand and squeezed it gently.

'Whatever you do, don't push until we tell you,' she advised. 'You're fully dilated. It shouldn't be long. Keep doing the breathing exercises. What's your name?' she went on with a smile.

'Sarah,' the sufferer told her weakly.

'Well, Sarah, you're soon going to be a mother for the second time.'

'Agh!' she cried. 'Let it be soon!'

'It will be,' Selina said. 'I can see the baby's head. Now, wait until I tell you, then push.'

'There's a layby straight ahead,' Kane said. 'I'm going to pull in there.'

Selina nodded.

'It's coming,' she told Sarah. 'Any moment now we're going to be in business.'

'Agh,' Sarah groaned. 'Can I push?'

'Yes! Now!' Kane's voice said from beside her, and as they eased the head out it was followed by the baby's shoulders, then the trunk and finally two tiny wrinkled legs.

'You have a daughter, Sarah,' Selina cried. 'A beautiful baby daughter!'

'Why isn't she crying?' the new mother cried anxiously.

Kane had picked the baby up, having clamped and cut the umbilicus, and was carefully patting it on the back, and as he did so a lusty yell issued forth. As the mother's sigh of relief echoed around the ambulance he passed the baby to her.

'Here, take your daughter, Sarah. The next thing we have to do is get you to hospital so that they can make sure the placenta comes away.'

His glance went to Selina. 'Are you all right?'

She nodded and he saw tears on her lashes.

'Yes,' she gulped. 'That was the most wonderful thing I've ever seen, watching the little one make its way out.'

His eyes were warm. 'Yes. Watching a child being born is incredible.'

Having seen the mother and child safely into the maternity unit a little later, they were about to leave when Sarah called them back.

'Can I ask you something?' she said with rising colour.

Her glance was on Selina who said immediately, 'Yes, of course. What is it?'

'What's your name?'

'My name?' she said.

'Yes. I'd like to call the baby after you, and I know that my husband will agree when he hears what's happened.'

'Er…it's Selina.'

Sarah smiled.

'That's a nice name. I'm glad it's not Maud or Matilda.' Amid shared laughter she went on, 'I'd thought of Joy if it was a girl. So that's what it will be—Selina Joy.'

'I really don't know what to say,' Selina breathed as pleasure washed over her. 'May I ask you to let us know when the christening is?'

'Yes, indeed,' Sarah said. 'I'd like you both as godparents. After all, you were the ones who brought her into the world. I'll ring the ambulance depot when we've set a date.'

A doctor with a midwife in attendance was looming up, and after a brief farewell Selina and Kane left.

When they reached the ambulance Selina said ecstatically, 'Wasn't that marvellous? My first birth and she's going to be called after me. We're going to be godparents, Kane!'

He was smiling across at her and, carried away by the moment, she put her arms around him and hugged him.

Accepting the gesture in the same light-hearted manner, he wasn't going to make anything out of it until he felt the curving softness of her up against him. He groaned.

'What's the matter?' she asked, her arms still around him.

'*You* are what's the matter,' he said flatly. 'I only need to touch you and I'm lost.'

'Oh, for goodness' sake, Kane!' she cried. 'Why do you have to make everything so difficult? We're both free agents. Well, you are anyway. *I've* got a child, who incidentally thinks you're great. We both do.'

'You've also got a band of protectors who won't want you to replace Dave with a stranger who has a seedy past.'

Selina was angry now.

'Rubbish! I'm quite capable of looking after my own affairs. Don't use Dave as an excuse to keep me on the edge of your life. You say that when you touch me you're lost. Well, see if you can find your way back from this.' And before he could move she was kissing him with a fierce tenderness that took his breath away, but only momentarily. His arms tightened around her, but Selina was stepping back.

'I'm sick of going round in circles, Kane,' she said flatly. 'Until you start treating me like an intelligent adult, that's it. And it's almost seven o'clock. Our shift finishes in a couple of minutes.'

He got into the ambulance and switched the engine on. As she slid into the seat beside him he said, 'I might surprise you one of these days and tell you all about it.'

'Really? Well, don't leave it too long—I might have found someone else by then.'

The closed expression was back again. 'That's up to you.'

And off they went back to the ambulance station and their separate ways.

As Selina drove back home, after picking Josh up, she was wishing she hadn't said such a stupid thing. It was childish and untrue to let Kane think her feelings for him were so shallow that she would be looking round for someone else if he didn't make things right between them.

Yet what about *his* feelings for *her*? He was no better, blowing hot and cold all the time.

But her face softened as she recalled what he'd said about his childhood and adolescence. She and Gavin had been cherished children. They'd never known insecurity and the lack of privacy Kane had described. He'd always had to fend for himself and it would seem that the hurt of having his life invaded and his integrity questioned had gone deep.

Thankfully, whatever it was that Charlie had heard about him hadn't become common knowledge at the station. She shuddered to think what he would be like if it did.

Was she being too trusting in her own attitude? she wondered. No, she wasn't. She loved him and was prepared to take Kane as she found him. Strong, reliable and caring.

There had been a thousand times when he could have taken advantage of her in the close confines of the ambulance if he'd wanted to, but she knew instinctively that he was the last person to do anything like that.

Sadly, *he* was the one causing the problems, with his stubborn pride and over-protectiveness.

'Have you seen Kane today?' Josh asked later as she was tucking him up for the night.

'Er…yes, of course. We're together all the time on the job, and guess what happened on my first day back? We delivered a baby girl and her parents are going to call her Selina after me. What do you think of that?'

He smiled up at her sleepily.

'Cool.'

Yes, it was 'cool', she thought as she went downstairs.

It had been a memorable experience that they'd almost blotted out by bickering afterwards.

That night Selina decided that she was going to apply to join the training course that preceded taking the exams to become a paramedic.

She didn't think Jill would mind as the hours that Josh was in her care would be fewer. The course took eight weeks, four of them at training school and the rest hospital-based. One of them was in Casualty. Two in theatre and one on the coronary unit.

It would give Kane and herself time apart. Time to see if they really did love each other. She had no doubts about her feelings, but his were far from clear.

She was aware that if she passed the exams the chances were that they wouldn't be working together any more, that she would be allocated a vehicle of her own with her own trainee to assist. But as the health authority only gave passes to those with the very top marks, she wasn't going to worry about that just yet.

You're a single parent, she reminded herself. Improving your qualifications has to be a good idea. Maybe you'll get the chance to be a fast-response paramedic if you qualify, and then you won't be involved with anybody.

She smiled wryly at her flights of fancy and then grimaced at the prospect of moving out of Kane's orbit, but something had to be done. They were getting nowhere fast.

When Kane found out that Selina had been to see the station officer about the paramedic course he said, 'Thanks for discussing it with me first.'

Still smarting from their conversation of the day before, she parried, 'So what's the problem? There seemed no point in mentioning it unless there was a chance of being accepted.'

'And?'

'He said he'd been wondering when I was going to get around to it.'

'So you're on?'

'It depends if there's a vacant place. They're going to let me know.'

'So we're not going to be seeing much of each other if they take you on.'

'No. It would seem not.'

'And you're not bothered?'

'Yes, of course I am, but what good does it do us when we're together? And in any case, why are you badgering me like this? You're the one who's been asking me when I was going to do something about qualifying.'

'I know, but I thought it was a decision we would make together.'

Her eyes widened in disbelief.

'Togetherness doesn't seem to be top of your list these days. That's why I thought I'd give separation a go.'

'I could shake you, Selina,' he said through gritted teeth.

'Really? Well, I suppose any kind of contact is better than none.'

'What's this I'm hearing?' Denise called across sarcastically. 'The Sugar Plum Fairy and Action Man having a disagreement? I don't believe it!'

That brought an end to the war of words and Selina was thankful that an emergency was coming through that was going to take them out into the city once more.

In the late evening of that same day Kane sat on the deck of *The Joshua*, gazing into space.

The nights were drawing in yet it was still warm and mellow. The golds and bronzes of autumn were beginning to appear and the fields around the village were ready for harvesting.

He had no regrets about coming to live in this place, whatever Selina might think. He had made the move to be near her…and to get away from the characterless flat. But even if she hadn't been close by, he would have been enchanted by his new surroundings.

At the moment he was appreciating them even more because if Selina was going to be away from the station for eight weeks, at least they would still be near each other when they were free of their work commitments.

But what was the point of being pleased about that when he was making such a mess of things? he wondered glumly. The way he was acting was totally out of character. He wasn't a ditherer. But, then, neither had he met anyone like Selina before.

It wouldn't be so bad if she hadn't been married previously and wasn't so vulnerable. Yet she was the one who had come to terms with that…and *he* was the one who was making it a problem.

He was crazy. If he had any sense he would get in touch with the authorities where he'd come from and ask for written proof that the inquiry had found him blameless.

But he couldn't do it. It was as if the very fact of feeling that he had to present proof of his innocence was a sign that he didn't have a clear conscience.

Yet Selina had made it clear that she had no problem with old gossip. Because that was the way she was, uncomplicated and trusting. But when it came down to basics, would she really want Josh to have a new father with morals that were suspect?

He might be the one spreading around the gloom, but *he* was also the one facing facts, and as Kane got up to pace restlessly along the deck he wasn't any nearer to a solution.

Selina had threatened to find someone else, but he knew her better than that. There was no spite in her. There was no spite in him either. All the problems in his life had been from the misdemeanours of others.

With a last look towards the lighted windows of her cottage, which were just visible on the skyline, he went slowly down to the cabin and his empty bunk.

There *was* a vacancy on the course and it was to commence the following Monday, so Selina had no time to change her mind or to think it over.

She'd made the decision on impulse and now must abide by it. From a career point of view it was wise thinking, and if Kane hadn't been in the background of her life she would have been raring to go.

As it was, she was torn between the challenge that it represented and the knowledge that they wouldn't be partners any more.

She knew deep down that he supported her resolve, but wasn't getting any pleasure from the thought of it. However, as she'd told herself a thousand times, he was the one who had to make the first move. She'd done all the pleading she was going to do.

The work during the first four weeks at training school was hard and exhausting. It was clear that the health authority wasn't prepared to allow its sick and injured to be treated by anyone who wasn't fully trained and competent, and as she took part in the exercises and ploughed through the text-books provided, Selina felt that it would be a miracle if she passed at the end of it.

Josh had been pleading to go to the boat, and as he wasn't old enough to go on his own she took him along the towpath one evening in the hope that they might find Kane at home.

She'd lost track of his working hours now that she was

no longer with him on the ambulance and so had no idea if he would be there.

Luckily he was, and pleasure coursed through her at the sight of him leaning over the side of the boat, watching them, as they approached.

As Josh scrambled onto the deck he was already asking, 'When can we go for a sail, Kane?'

He ruffled the boy's fair mop with a big, capable hand, and smiling down at him, he said, 'Why don't we *all* go for a sail? The three of us? Your mum hasn't yet got her water legs.'

'I don't think so,' she muttered, backing away.

She was supposed to be distancing herself from him and a sail in the autumn evening with Kane so close would hardly be that.

'Yes! Yes!' Josh cried. 'Come on, Mum!'

The man by his side was eyeing her quizzically as if he could read her mind. He held out a hand to her and waited, and as Josh cried again, 'Come on, Mum,' she stepped on board.

'So how's the course going?' Kane asked as the engine came to life and he manoeuvred the boat smoothly out of the marina and into the middle of the canal.

She pulled a face.

'It's hard. Very hard! I don't think I'll pass.'

Kane smiled. 'So I might get my partner back after all. I'm with a trainee at the moment and he's useless.'

'You don't really want me to fail, do you?' she said with hurt in her eyes.

'No, of course not. I was just teasing. You'll make a great paramedic.'

'Hmm. We'll see.'

Selina's gaze was on the scene before her. The banks were covered in willow trees and wild flowers and there were ducks flying over in perfect formation.

He was following her glance.

'Those fellows belong to the nature park, I'm told. They fly over every evening.'

Her eyes were dreamy. She was glad she'd come.

'Everywhere I look there's beauty,' she breathed.

'Same here,' he agreed, but, entranced by the scenery around her, Selina wasn't aware that he was referring to a beauty visible only to himself.

He was seeing violet eyes, smooth skin tinted the palest gold and the bright swathe of her hair lifting gently in the breeze from the water.

Suddenly she became aware of the intensity of his regard and, swivelling to face him, asked, 'What?'

'This,' he said with equal brevity. And drawing her towards him, he took her in his arms.

In the last few moments their attention hadn't been on Josh playing around at the back of the boat and round the cabin, but it was on him quickly enough when there was a frightened cry and a splash as he hit the water.

'Josh!' she screamed as Kane's arms fell away to cut the engine and peel off his sweater.

'Can he swim?' he cried as he stood poised to jump.

'Just a little. He's only just started learning.'

She was talking to space. All she could see were Kane's heels as he followed her son into the dark green waters of the canal.

Gasping and spluttering, Josh had surfaced, and before he was dragged down again Kane had him in a secure grip. The water wasn't all that deep, but Selina knew there would be weeds and algae below the surface which could drag them down.

Kane was holding onto the side of the boat with one hand and grasping Josh with the other, and when Selina saw the reeds and slime on them she knew that her surmise hadn't been wrong.

She reached over and grabbed Josh's arm with an urgency born of sheer panic and then, with Kane hoisting him up from behind and herself dragging him over the edge of the boat, he was sprawled on the deck.

Kane already had one leg over the edge and shortly afterwards he, too, was dripping all over the boards.

'Mum, I'm going to be sick,' Josh said. 'I've swallowed some water and it tasted horrible!'

She was down the stairs, into the galley and back up again with a bowl in her hands quicker than the speed of light, and as he bent over it Kane looked down at himself and said ruefully, 'So much for the beauty around us. Do you fancy carrying on where we left off?'

She wrinkled her nose.

'I think not,' she told him as the tears that were threatening turned to laughter. 'You're a smelly pair.'

Kane masterfully regained control of the boat and steered it back towards the marina. Josh's nausea had passed but he still looked green from every angle and Selina told them, 'We need to get you both to hospital. There's no telling what you could pick up from the water that you've swallowed. It will be full of bacteria.'

'OK,' Kane agreed, 'but first we need to get out of these clothes and under the shower.'

'Yes, and then you can have a hug for services rendered,' she told him, her eyes tender. 'I don't know how we managed to cope before you came along.'

'You did, though, didn't you?'

'After a fashion,' she conceded. She took Josh by the hand. 'We're going home so this young man can get cleaned up. Will you pick us up when you're ready?'

As the boat bumped to a stop by the marina wall, he sighed.

'Yes. I'll be round in twenty minutes. What an ending to what could have been a perfect evening.'

'Indeed,' she agreed wistfully. 'Maybe the fates are trying to tell us something.'

They gave Josh a thorough examination in A and E and the verdict was that he seemed all right, apart from the nausea that was still persisting.

'I suggest a course of antibiotics for you both,' the doctor in charge said, 'and with a bit of luck you won't have any after-effects from the canal water.'

When they arrived back at the house Selina said, 'Come in and have a coffee with us, Kane.'

He shook his head.

'Thanks, but, no, Selina. The boat's in a filthy mess. I need to do some cleaning up.'

'All right, then, but before you leave us there's a promise I must keep.'

'And what's that?'

'I owe you a hug.' And before he could move she put her arms around him once more, kissed him gently on the cheek and said softly, 'Thank you for what you did tonight.'

It was the moment to tell her that cleaning the boat was an excuse, that he couldn't trust himself to be alone with her without abandoning his scruples.

But he could hear Josh calling for her and Selina was waving goodbye and closing the door. Telling himself that the boy needed her more than he did, Kane went on his solitary way.

Josh didn't suffer any ill effects from his dip in the canal and Selina assumed that Kane had been equally fortunate.

It was an assumption that lasted until a couple of days later when Jill called round to say, 'I forgot to mention when you picked Josh up after work that the local GP was visiting your friend Kane this afternoon. I'd taken the children to the park and on our way back we saw the doctor going on board.'

Selina had gone pale. Was he ill? He had to be if he'd called the doctor out. And if he was, who was looking after him? Nobody. He was all alone on *The Joshua*.

'I'll go round,' she said immediately, to Jill's amusement. 'It will either be chickenpox or some sort of gastric bug after the canal episode. I'll bet he wishes us far away. We bring him nothing but trouble.'

'I don't somehow think that Kane sees it like that, from what you've told me about him,' her sister-in-law said laughingly. 'You're a dream girl, Selina. Any man who gets you will be a lucky guy.'

'There's only one guy I want,' Selina said pensively, 'and he's not falling over himself to do anything about it.'

When she felt the deck of *The Joshua* beneath her feet Selina was suddenly nervous. There was no movement on board, no noise, just silence.

Supposing Jill was wrong, that it hadn't been the doctor she'd seen. Kane would think she was crazy, rushing round to check up on him if her sister-in-law had been mistaken. She called his name and it echoed back at her eerily.

As she hesitated at the top of the stairs that led to the cabin below she thought, Supposing he isn't alone. What do I do then? Yet surely if that was the case someone would have answered her call.

Kane was asleep on one of the two bunks that provided the sleeping arrangements on the boat, and as Selina drew nearer she saw that his face was swollen. The skin was bright red and scaly and it was the same on his arms and neck. His breathing was erratic also and every few seconds he made a wheezing noise.

Guilt washed over her. He looked dreadful. Whatever was wrong with him, it had to be from the other night.

There was a prescription for antibiotics on top of the locker beside the bed, but obviously he hadn't felt up to going to the chemist to have it made up.

She picked it up and as she stood with it in her hand she knew that somehow or other she had to find a chemist. But why had the G.P. prescribed more antibiotics? He wouldn't have finished the first course yet.

'Too late,' he croaked suddenly. 'They'll be closed.'

'I thought you were asleep,' she said anxiously. 'What's wrong, Kane? You look awful.'

'I feel it,' he said groggily. 'I called the doctor out this afternoon and he says that the tablets they gave me at the hospital are penicillin-based and it appears that I'm allergic to it.'

'Didn't you know you were allergic?' she asked in surprise.

'No,' he croaked. 'I've never had anything wrong with me before. The prescription in your hand is for a different kind of antibiotic that hasn't got penicillin in it, but it felt like too much effort to go and get it made up.'

'Why didn't you let me know you were feeling like this? she said worriedly. 'For one thing, I'm to blame. I should have taken more note of what Josh was up to, instead of letting you distract me. If you hadn't had to jump in the canal after him, you wouldn't have needed the drug.'

'Yes, I know,' he said impatiently, 'but those sorts of accidents come out of the blue. It was nobody's fault. And I'll soon throw this off. I'm rarely ill.'

'That may be so,' she persisted, 'but don't play it down. I've heard of people who've died from a reaction to penicillin. I had a friend who started with some kind of bug and she remembered that she had some tablets in the bathroom cupboard. They'd been there for a long time and when she took one it nearly killed her. She ended up in Intensive Care and—'

He groaned. 'All right. I admit that I feel ghastly.'

'Yes, I can tell. That's why I'm off to get this prescription made up. You can't go through the night without something to counteract the allergy. I'll be back the moment I've sorted it. There's an all-night chemist near the city centre.'

Selina's voice rose. 'The doctor who came this afternoon should have made sure you could get it made up when he saw that you were on your own. In fact, he should have had you admitted to hospital.'

'I didn't tell him I lived alone and when he mentioned hospital I said I'd rather see how it went once I was on the new tablets.'

'I see. In other words, you've got a death wish?'

Kane managed a grimace of a smile.

'Not now I haven't. I'm looking forward to having your cool hand on my fevered brow.'

'You're going to have to wait, I'm afraid,' she told him. 'Getting your prescription made up is going to do more for your fevered brow than my cool hand.' And as he sank back against the pillows the alarm that had been there from the moment of seeing him on the bunk became an urgent need to make him well again.

Don't let anything happen to Kane, she prayed as she drove out of the village. He was making light of it, but they both knew that this kind of allergic reaction could be very serious.

The chemist had been open. The new tablets were on the seat beside her, and as Selina made the return journey along roads that were quiet after the evening rush hour she was deciding what she was going to do.

First the patient must be given the treatment, then she was going to pick Josh up from Gavin's house where she'd left him for what she'd thought would be a few moments.

And once she'd packed some nightwear they were both going back to the boat.

When she got back Kane was in the same feverish doze she'd found him in earlier, and his skin was so red and flaky it looked as if he'd been in the hot sun.

As she touched him gently on the shoulder he muttered, 'What is it, Eve? Leave me alone.'

Selina stared down at him. She was still in his mind, the woman who'd caused him so much aggravation.

'Sit up for a moment, Kane,' she coaxed gently.

As he eased himself up on the pillows, he said blearily, 'You're back.'

She managed a smile.

'Yes, and my name isn't Eve.'

'I'm not with you.'

'No. You're not,' she agreed, 'but maybe if you take the medication you'll find yourself coming back from wherever you've been. And, Kane, I'm going to have to leave you again for a few minutes while I go to get Josh.'

'Don't worry about me any more, Selina,' he protested. 'I'll be all right now I've got the new tablets. I think my immune system is beginning to kick in too. I don't feel quite so much as if I'm going to choke.'

'The choking and breathing problems will be because the allergy has made the membranes of your mouth and throat swell, and I'll be the judge of whether you're well enough to be left,' she said firmly.

Josh needed no persuasion. The thought of spending the night on the boat had him jumping up and down with glee.

'Where will I sleep?' he asked as they approached the marina. 'In one of the bunks?'

'Yes. Kane is in one and you can have the other.'

'But where are you going to sleep, Mum?' he asked.

'I'll want to keep awake,' she told him. 'Kane is quite poorly and I want to be there if he needs me.'

That described her feelings for Kane exactly, she thought as she tucked Josh up in the other bunk. She wanted to be there for him, not just now but always...in sickness and in health. But so far it seemed to be a one-sided state of affairs.

She woke him up for another tablet at one o'clock in the morning and when he saw the time Kane said, 'Selina! Have you seen the time? You shouldn't be here at this hour.'

'You mean, what will the neighbours say?' she teased.

'No. I mean, who's looking after Josh?'

'Cast your eyes sideways.'

He did and they nearly popped out.

'He's spending his first night aboard and totally happy to do so.'

Kane groaned. 'Ugh! What a nuisance I'm being.'

'No, you're not. How long is it since you had some TLC?'

'Too far back to remember.'

'So don't knock it when it's offered.'

'Yes, but—'

Selina shook her head chidingly. 'Shush. I'm not leaving you until you look less like a lobster.'

He groaned again. 'Do I look that bad?'

''Fraid so. Eve would definitely not fancy you at this moment.'

'And what about you?'

'Oh, I fancy you all the time, but it doesn't seem to be getting me anywhere.'

He smiled wearily.

'I notice that you only tell me that when I'm not able to act upon it.'

'There's no rush,' she said quietly as he closed his eyes again. 'Just get better, Kane.'

CHAPTER EIGHT

WHEN she awoke huddled on one of the seats in the cabin in an autumn dawn, Selina realised that she must have slept after all.

As consciousness came flooding back her first thought was for Kane. His bunk was empty, and as she got to her feet she could see the outline of him under the shower in the boat's small bathroom.

It was half past six. In two hours she would have to be on her way to the training school, but only if he was well enough for her to leave him.

She went into the galley and put the kettle on and then went slowly up on deck. When Kane came out of the shower she would know soon enough how he was, and in the meantime, as an early sun came slanting across the marina, she was experiencing the pleasure of life on the water.

Everywhere was still. A kingfisher on the far bank observed her in feathered brilliance, and a water rat stood poised for flight at the slightest sound.

'There you are,' Kane said suddenly from behind her, and when she turned he was there, with a towel draped across his shoulders and the bottom half of him covered by boxer shorts.

'Do I still look like a lobster?' he asked as her glance took in the casual lean grace of him.

Selina smiled to disguise the ache that his semi-nakedness had caused. He looked clean and wholesome, while she was a creased and crumpled mess.

126

'Not as much,' she said lightly. 'You've gone from red to pink. Am I to take it that you're feeling better?'

'Yes, you are. I'm relieved to say. The new medication seems to be doing the trick. I don't ever want a repeat performance of that little episode. But, of course, I shall know in future that penicillin is not for me.'

'So we've got something in common,' she said, with a feeling of anticlimax now the anxiety was past.

'Who? You and I?'

'No. Penicillin and myself.'

'Huh?'

'Neither of us suit you.'

He took a step towards her and the towel fell from his shoulders.

'Don't spoil it, Selina,' he said soberly as his nearness made her tremble. 'You "suit" me very well. I've never been better "suited" in my life. But our backgrounds and circumstances are so different. You are a cherished innocent and I'm streetwise and cynical. Not the best mix for everlasting bliss.'

'You're making excuses,' she said flatly. 'I have my own opinion of what you're like and I don't want your version rammed down my throat. I'm going to get Josh up, and once he's dressed we'll be off.'

'Surely not before I've thanked you properly for taking care of me.'

'I would have done it for anyone,' she told him in the same flat tone.

Josh was loud in his protests when he discovered that they were leaving almost as soon as he was awake.

'We have to go home,' she told him patiently. 'I'm due at the training centre at nine o'clock and I have to take you round to Uncle Gavin's house first.'

'Can't I stay here with Kane?' he pleaded.

'*I* don't mind,' Kane said, turning from the window

where he'd been gazing morosely over the water. 'I'm going to ring in sick today.'

Selina hesitated as her concern for him outweighed her annoyance.

'No, Kane. You're only partly recovered. You can't throw off that sort of thing in a day. Josh is coming with me.'

'All right, if that's how you feel,' he conceded. Turning to the boy who was eyeing his mother mutinously, he said, 'There'll be another time, Josh. I promise.'

Not for us, Selina thought bleakly a little later as she gave Josh his breakfast back at the house. There won't be another time for us if you keep on like this, my dear one.

When Selina arrived home that evening there was a huge bouquet of flowers in the porch. She picked it up slowly and read the card attached.

It said, 'You wouldn't let me thank you this morning so I'm hoping this will do it for me. I'm sure you'll find them more pleasing than their sender.'

Her eyes filled with tears. What was the matter with the man? He was all she would ever want, but for some reason he was determined to continue the pattern of past deprivation that he'd once casually mentioned. His determination was such that getting him to change his mind was like coming up against a brick wall.

Yet she needed to know how he was—if the improvement was continuing—and a call to his mobile seemed the most painless way of finding out.

'Yes, I'm still improving,' Kane said when he answered. 'How has your day been?'

'It didn't have a very good start,' she told him pointedly, 'but it got better as it went on. Thank you for the flowers. They are lovely. But, Kane…'

'What?' he said guardedly.

'If you sent me a thousand bouquets it wouldn't make up for what you're doing to us.'

There was silence, ominous and complete, and then at last his voice came over the line again and it brought a chill with it.

'Look, Selina, it's hard enough to keep away from you. Don't keep making an issue of it. Good luck with the course. I'll see you when it's over.'

As the line went dead she stood looking down at the receiver in her hand. If that wasn't telling her to keep her distance, she didn't know what was. He'd said he would see her after the course. In other words, when she reported back for duty at the ambulance station. So the fact that they lived only minutes apart didn't come into it.

He hadn't said it in so many words but the meaning was clear. Stay away from me, he was telling her.

Well, she thought angrily, she would do just that. It wouldn't please Josh, but did she want to store up misery for her son? Better he should forget about Kane. Better they should both forget about him.

Kane was back on the job the next morning. For one thing he was feeling much better, and for another the last thing he wanted to do was mope around the boat, thinking about Selina.

His breathing was back to normal. The swollen membranes in his mouth and throat had gone down and his skin had lost its extreme redness. Those were the physical improvements.

Mentally he was still suffering and it wasn't anything to do with the adverse effects of penicillin. But having decided on the road he was going to travel, he might as well get on with it, he told himself, and as the ambulance station came into view he was preparing himself for another busy day.

It wasn't the same without her, of course. Selina was in a class of her own. Quietly efficient, kind, caring and strong in her own way. But, then, she would have to be to contemplate sharing her life with the likes of him.

Maybe he ought to ask to be put on one of the fast-response vehicles. That way he would be on his own and that was how he performed best...wasn't it?

As the weeks went by it was still stalemate between them, with Selina now training in the various sections of the hospital, Kane coping with urban emergencies and Josh occasionally getting upset at not being allowed near the boat.

To make up for it Selina took him to all the other things he liked doing—cinema, zoo, a nearby theme park—and on the surface he seemed content.

All of which was becoming a regular pattern until the day that Josh and the twins disappeared.

When Selina went to pick him up at her sister-in-law's after a gruelling day in Coronary Care, she found Jill totally distraught.

'I can't find the children anywhere!' she cried. 'They were playing in the garden half an hour ago and when I went out to check on them they weren't there. I've looked everywhere. Back at your place. The park. The post office in case they'd sneaked off to buy some sweets. But there isn't a sign of them!'

Selina was staring at her in dismayed disbelief.

'They can't be far away, Jill,' she said evenly, knowing that one of them panicking was enough.

A clear head and calm mind were required in situations such as this, but it wasn't stopping fear clutching at her as all the awful possibilities came crowding in.

'Gavin's at the hospital. There's only been me here,' Jill sobbed, 'and I've been running round like someone demented. Suppose...suppose...'

'Shush!' Selina told her. 'Let's not suppose anything at the moment. You're overwrought. We'll both start searching in opposite directions. Three small children can't move that fast.'

Jill wiped her eyes with the back of her hand.

'I don't know about that. Children can move like greased lightning when they want to go somewhere, and you know what the girls are like. They would jump in the canal if Josh told them to.'

'The canal!' they both breathed simultaneously.

'Supposing he's taken them to see Kane?' Selina said. 'Let's go!'

As they ran along the towpath she was wondering whether he would be there. He might be if he was on nights as he didn't start until seven. Or they might find him there if it was one of his days off. But if he was on a day shift he would be absent as he didn't finish until seven. In any case, if the children had turned up at the boat he would have brought them straight back.

When they came to a breathless halt beside *The Joshua* it was clear that they'd come on a fruitless errand. It was all locked up and there was no sign of the man himself.

Jill was weeping again.

'This is all my fault,' she wailed. 'I should have kept a better watch on them.'

'No, don't blame yourself,' Selina told her as her own hopes were dashed. She put her arm around her sister-in-law's shaking shoulders. 'There's no one more careful than you. Let's go back and see if they've turned up.'

Two hours later they were again searching the places they'd already looked. There had been no signs of the children when they'd got back and Jill had phoned to ask Gavin to come home.

He had taken charge of the search and now, with no success to report, he was about to phone the police.

'We can't take any chances,' he told his distraught wife and sister, 'in case they've been abducted. The police need to know so that they can watch all the roads for suspicious vehicles. The first few hours after an abduction are vital.'

His face was bleached of all colour, but he'd had to say it. Just in case...

Selina wanted to scream at him. Don't say that word! I can't bear to think of it. Yet she knew he was right.

'The police are coming right over,' he said as he put the phone down after the call. 'Selina, I suggest that you stay here to talk to them when they arrive and Jill and I will continue searching.' Before she could argue they'd gone.

It had been one of those days. An entrapment. A multiple pile-up on the motorway. A schoolboy with burns after trying to make a firework bomb. By the time it was over Kane was ready for a couple of hours' relaxation in a bar near the ambulance station.

There was nothing to rush home for. The boat would manage without its owner for a little while longer. It was still a great source of pleasure, but he always took a nightly stroll past Lock-Keeper's Cottage. Even though his dreams had taken a wrong turning...

It was almost ten o'clock when he got back to the village. All the lights were on when he went past Selina's house and his face tightened when he saw the garage fellow come hurrying out.

It looked as if she and the mechanic had been having a cosy night in, he thought, and had to swerve as a police car came speeding past.

There was another one parked beside the village green and he thought that there seemed to be a lot of activity in the area. But as it didn't concern him he was going to turn in as soon as he was back on the boat and sleep off the stress of a long and tiring day.

When he went to get the keys, which he kept hidden in a small cavity beneath the door of the cabin, they weren't there. He eyed the empty space in perplexity. Were there thieves about? Was that the reason for all the police activity?

Yet there were no signs of a break-in. All appeared to be in order. The door that led to the accommodation below was securely locked and the windows closed, though he supposed that someone could have been prowling around, found the keys and taken them with the intention of coming back later.

He sighed. This was all he needed. He was going to have to break in, either smash a window or force the door. He peered downwards through the glass panel in the door and his jaw went slack.

In the light of a lamp on the banks of the marina and the beams of a full moon he could dimly see small figures curled up on the bunks. Three of them. And he recognised one of them as the only other person who knew where he kept the key. Josh!

At that moment it all became clear. The police presence. The fellow from the garage hurrying out of Selina's house where all the lights were blazing out into the autumn night.

He banged on the door and bellowed the boy's name, and Josh stirred sleepily. Kane called again and this time he sat up on the bunk and looked fearfully upwards.

When he saw Kane peering down at him he came slowly up the steps.

'Josh! Where's the key?' he cried.

Josh opened a grubby fist and it was there in the middle of his palm.

'Open the door!' Kane ordered.

The boy rubbed his eyes with the back of his hand. 'I can't. It's stuck.'

'No, it's not,' Kane said, calmer now that he had the situation in hand. 'It's a special lock and it can be tricky. Open one of the windows and pass the key to me, and I'll have you out in no time.'

At that moment Katy and Kristy appeared behind him and when they saw Kane's shadow at the door their mouths opened wide and screams issued forth.

'Hurry,' he told Josh. 'The girls are frightened.'

With the key once more in his possession, it was an easy matter to release the three small fugitives. The moment they were up on deck the wailing stopped.

'Right, Josh,' he said quietly as the children eyed him apprehensively. 'Now, tell me what this is all about.'

Selina's son took a deep breath.

'I brought the girls to play on our boat and when we got here they wanted to see inside, but it was locked.'

'And you just happened to know where the key was?'

'Yes,' he admitted, looking down at the deck.

'And?'

'When we got into the cabin I shut the door behind us and it locked and we couldn't get out.'

'I see. So even though you had the key in your hand, you couldn't open the door?'

'Yes,' he muttered. 'It was all right at first, hiding down there, but when it began to go dark we didn't know what to do.'

Kane reached for his mobile.

'Yes?' Selina's voice croaked hopefully when he got through.

'It's Kane here,' he said, and got no further.

'I can't talk now,' she babbled. 'Something terrible has happened. Josh and the twins are missing.'

'Not any more,' he said gently. 'I've just found them in

the cabin on my boat. Three little castaways, desperate to see their mums.'

'Oh! Thank goodness!' she choked. 'We'll be right there. I've been living in a nightmare for the last few hours.'

'I take it that's why the police are in the village.'

'Yes,' she said hurriedly. 'I'm off to find Jill and Gavin, Kane. Don't let those little scallywags out of your sight.'

He sighed.

'As if I would.'

He felt guilty about the whole thing. If he hadn't taken Josh to his heart, like he had, the child wouldn't be so interested in the boat…and if he'd come straight home from work Selina would have been saved hours of anguish.

Whatever he did, wherever he turned, he was involved in her life in one way or another, and it hurt a lot because he was reluctantly trying to achieve the opposite.

He stood to one side as the children were reunited with their ecstatic parents, and hid a smile at the way the three of them had bounced back as if it had been a great adventure instead of a frightening experience.

Selina met his glance above her son's tousled head and the promise of what they could all be to each other was in her eyes. He felt himself weaken. She was the most beautiful thing he'd ever seen and he'd dithered long enough.

It was at that moment that the police arrived, straight-faced, officious. Incredibly, they questioned him as if he was up to no good.

Had the children been on the boat when he'd left? Was he responsible for them being locked up? What had been his intentions when he'd got back?

'I'd intended going to bed,' he told them stonily, 'after doing a twelve-hour shift with the ambulance service.'

'And can anyone vouch for you being on the job all the time?'

'Yes. The lad who was with me.'

Selina was listening, aghast.

'Kane is a close family friend,' she told the officer who was asking the questions, 'and in any case the children were with my sister-in-law until late afternoon.'

The officer had put away his notebook.

'That will be all, then, sir,' he said imperturbably. 'We've heard what the boy has to say, but as you will know we have to be very careful where the disappearance of children is concerned.'

'Of course,' Kane replied with cold politeness, and wondered when the demon that seemed to be forever on his shoulder was going to go away.

When parents, children and the constabulary had gone, quietness settled over the boat once more and, with sleep forgotten, Kane stood on deck, gazing sombrely over the marina.

Why was it that he who led a blameless life should always be on the fringe of something nasty? he asked himself grimly. He felt like packing his bags and going as far away as he could get. But if he did that he would never see Selina again and he wasn't into self-punishment to that extent.

His phone rang at that moment. It was Selina.

'Are you all right, Kane?' she asked anxiously.

'Yes,' he said abruptly, then added in a softer tone, 'Are you? You've had a dreadful experience.'

'Yes, it was. One always thinks the worst, we kept wondering if the children had been abducted.'

'By someone like me, you mean?'

'No. I don't mean that at all. You are a rock in my life.'

'Really? Rocks aren't always the safest things to cling to, you know. Goodnight, Selina. Sleep well. You've got your boy back.' And before she could try to comfort him further he rang off.

*   *   *

Selina was drained as she finally climbed the stairs to bed.
It had been a day she wouldn't forget in a hurry. One nightmare after another. The anguish of the children being lost
and then the policeman's questioning of Kane.

It was no wonder he wasn't feeling too happy, and she
didn't blame him. It couldn't have happened to anyone less
deserving, even though the policeman had only been doing
his job.

Kane carried his pride like a huge chip on his shoulder.
The life he'd lived had made him that way. But was he
going to let it spoil things for them? It looked very much
like it.

Each day when she awoke she dreaded that they would
find *The Joshua* gone the next time they went along the
towpath. And who could blame Kane if he did pull up
sticks?

There'd been the night when she'd insisted that he tell
her about himself, and what had happened afterwards, and
though she'd done her best to show him that she was prepared to take him as she found him, it hadn't seemed to
make any difference.

Then, to cap it all, and insensitive beyond belief, the
interrogation on the boat tonight.

For goodness' sake! He'd been the one who'd found the
children…and it was Josh's yearning to be near Kane and
the boat that had pointed his feet in that direction.

Selina passed a weary hand over her brow. She could go
over it all until she was blue in the face, but it wasn't going
to change anything.

After Dave had died there had been no intent in her to
find someone to take his place. Yet it had happened. She'd
fallen in love totally and completely, and had hoped that
Kane might feel the same, but his pride was wrapped
around him like armour and so far she hadn't been able to
pierce it.

Take one day at a time, she told herself as she slumped onto the bed. And maybe… She was slipping over the edge into an exhausted sleep and 'maybe' was shelved until another day.

'Is Kane angry with me?' Josh asked as the days went by with no sign of him.

'No, of course not,' Selina told him.

'Is he angry with you, then?'

'No,' she said again. 'He isn't. I think he's more angry with himself than anyone.'

Perplexed blue eyes met hers.

'But he hasn't done anything wrong.'

'No, he hasn't. It might be better if he had,' she said abstractedly, which left Josh even more confused.

The paramedic course was progressing and when Selina came home each day she felt that if the exams were as difficult as the course, she wouldn't be in charge of her own vehicle for some time to come.

Peter was still hovering, and though she'd been glad of his support on the night the children had gone missing her feelings towards him hadn't changed.

'It would have to be lover boy who found the kids,' he'd snapped when he'd heard about Kane finding them on the boat. 'If you hadn't let Josh go round there so much it wouldn't have happened.'

Selina hadn't taken him up on it. She knew what ailed him and didn't want to know about it. When he'd gone stomping off she'd thought that little did he know that Kane wasn't her lover. She wished he was. And he was certainly no boy. He was a man. Every inch of him.

For someone who'd been accused of sexual harassment Kane wasn't exactly falling over himself to make love to her, which made her all the more convinced that he was a man who didn't spread his favours around…or force himself on others. Far from it!

If their relationship went on like it was doing, she might find herself seducing *him*. There were times when she let her imagination run riot, when she dreamt of standing before him in pliant nakedness and Kane forgetting all his hang-ups as he gave in to their need for each other.

But that was all they were, dreams. Life in its present form was made up of work, worry and wistful longing.

The results of the exams were out and Selina had passed. She'd actually passed! She was now a fully fledged paramedic. Not all that much better off financially, but when it came to status, a big step up the ladder.

The first thing she wanted to do when the glad tidings had been absorbed was to tell her colleagues at the ambulance station, Kane especially. This was something separate from their private lives. It was about the job…healthcare…and what it meant to them.

As she left the training centre, Philip Bassett, one of the instructors who'd been on the course, came up to her. He was from down south and seemed a bit like a fish out of water in his new surroundings.

'Well done, Selina,' he said with a congratulatory handshake. 'I hope that if ever I need an ambulance, you'll be on board.'

She smiled. 'Let's hope that won't be for a long time.'

He shrugged. 'If loneliness were an illness, I'd be needing healthcare already. I moved up here to be near my sister, and I'd no sooner got settled in than she died. I don't know a soul and I'm due to retire soon.'

'Oh, dear. That is sad,' she said. 'Why don't you come round to my place some time? I'm a widow with a nine-year-old son and my social life isn't exactly flourishing.'

Philip's face lit up. 'That's very kind. I'd love to.'

'Give me a ring some time and we'll fix up a date. I'm back on shifts next week, of course, but we can sort something out.' With a smile she added, 'We northern folk can't have you thinking we're low on hospitality.'

'Whatever you say,' he agreed, and after exchanging phone numbers they parted.

It was midday and as Selina drove to the ambulance centre she was willing Kane to be there, though there was nothing to guarantee that he would be. Even if he was on days he might be stationed somewhere in the city or have gone out on a call straight from base.

When she arrived, with eyes sparkling and a smile lighting up her face, one of the men called across, 'What are *you* doing here, Selina? I thought you were on a course.'

'I am…I mean, I was,' she told him. 'I've passed. I'm a paramedic!'

The shout went up.

'Congratulations!'

'Thanks,' she said absently.

She was looking around for Kane but it seemed as if she was to be disappointed.

'So, are we going for a drink to celebrate?' someone suggested, and before she could say yes or no it had been arranged that they would meet at the nearest wine bar at the end of the day shift.

She wasn't all that keen on the idea as it would mean going back home to change and asking Jill to have Josh for a while longer, but there had been so much genuine pleasure on her behalf amongst those she worked with that it would have been hard to refuse.

Mark Guthrie had already been informed that she'd passed and he called her into his office for a chat.

'This is good news, Selina,' he told her. 'You deserve the upgrade. When you come back to us next week you'll have one of the trainees with you and we'll take it from there.'

'So I won't be with Kane any more?'

'Well, no. We like to spread the paramedics out, one of them to each trainee.'

As she came out of the office she was telling herself that she'd known that was how it would be, yet she'd still asked the question.

When she went back to the rest room Kane was there. It seemed that he was a member of one of two crews who'd just got back from emergencies. As the new arrivals crowded round her to hear her news he stood to one side, watching her with a grave intensity that made her want to go across and shake him.

Didn't he see that he was the only one she wanted to hear from? she thought wretchedly. Everyone was being so kind and he was standing there as if he'd been struck dumb.

She wasn't to know it, but that was the case. Kane was speechless. He hadn't seen her in days, weeks even, and his need of her was so rampant he couldn't think straight.

He'd expected her to qualify. Selina was good, one of the best he'd ever worked with, and he was extremely pleased at her success. But it was as if he'd lost the power of speech.

The group around her was breaking up and with one long level look in his direction she was ready to go.

'I'll see you all tonight,' she called from the doorway, and as he wondered what that was about, she went.

As Selina drove home there was a bleak sort of resignation inside her. Kane was not only stingy with his affections, he was also not forthcoming with congratulations either. Surely he didn't begrudge her the success she'd worked for. If he did it was mean-minded, and she had been way out in her judgement.

His behaviour had taken the edge off her excitement and

Josh's words came to mind. He'd wanted to know if Kane was angry with them and she'd told him stoutly that he wasn't. Maybe she'd been mistaken. He was always getting caught up in their lives and perhaps he'd had enough.

The outskirts of the village were in sight, and as she pulled up in front of her brother's house domestic matters had to take over from affairs of the heart.

Josh and the twins were watching TV when she went inside, and she was able to take Jill to one side to tell her the good news.

'That's wonderful!' Jill cried. 'What did Kane have to say?'

'Nothing.'

'What do you mean—nothing?'

'Even Denise Hapgood congratulated me, but he just stood and stared.'

'How long is it since you've seen each other?'

'Ages.'

'Well, there you are,' Jill pronounced triumphantly. 'He's afraid of saying the wrong thing.'

'I doubt it. He's got that off to a fine art.'

'What?'

'Saying the wrong thing.'

'So there's no progress.'

'No. None.'

'Then the guy has to be blind,' Jill teased.

CHAPTER NINE

THE phone rang as Selina was getting changed for the evening ahead, and her throat went dry when Kane's voice came over the line.

'Selina?'

After the episode earlier in the afternoon there was no way she was going to let him know that just the sound of his voice was bliss. It was the lack of that very thing that had put her in the doldrums ever since.

So she said drily, 'Oh, you *can* speak, then. Or perhaps your silence, when everyone was falling over themselves to congratulate me, was because every time you open your mouth you put your foot in it?'

'Maybe it was,' he said, 'and as I take size nines, you have to agree it's quite a "feet".'

'Very funny. I'm glad you can find something to joke about. But what can I do for you? I'm sure you haven't just rung to tell me the size of your feet.'

He was serious now. He knew she had every right to be annoyed after his ridiculous behaviour that afternoon and flippancy wasn't going to mend matters.

'No. I haven't. I'll take you to the wine bar if you like. As we live so close it seems silly for us both to drive into the city. What have you done about Josh?'

'He's staying with Gavin and Jill for the night.'

'So you don't have to hurry back.'

'No, not if I don't want to,' she said stiffly, wondering where all this was leading. 'But I'm not intending to stay too late.'

'Of course. That's up to you. So, am I picking you up?'

'No, you're not!' she told him. 'You don't have to patronise me because you can't find it in you to be glad that I've passed my exams.'

'All right, Selina, if that's how you feel,' he said levelly. 'We seem to be running true to form. You in the right all the time and I in the wrong. I'll see you there.'

Her defiance lasted until she found that her car wouldn't start. As she stood beside it, fuming, the darkened garage down the road showed that it was no use going for Peter, and she was certainly not going to eat humble pie where Kane was concerned.

It wasn't in her nature to feel like this, she thought miserably. If only he would give in and tell her he loved her. But maybe he didn't. Perhaps she was taking too much for granted.

Her dilemma was about to be solved. Kane's car was coming along the road towards her and, on seeing her standing forlornly beside her own non-starter, he stopped and got out.

'What's the problem?' he asked briefly.

'I think the battery might be flat.'

'Right. You'd better let me give you that lift after all, then, hadn't you?'

'I suppose so.'

'Or would you rather phone for a taxi as I'm so low in your esteem?'

'No. I'll come with you...just as long as you take note that it's on sufferance.'

He nodded, and as she observed his profile in the darkening night she saw that he was smiling.

During the drive into the city Selina's glance was on his hands, resting loosely on the steering-wheel. They'd had a discussion earlier about his feet, without any great excitement on her part, but the rest of him was a different matter and she knew just how much she longed for him to touch her.

'What?' he asked suddenly, and she hoped he hadn't read her mind.

'Nothing.'

'Who's short on words now?'

'Ha. Ha.'

He pulled up at the side of the dark country lane that led to the main highway, and as she eyed him questioningly he said, 'Look, Selina, let's not bicker all night. You should know that I of all people wish you well in your career. I was the one who told you to go for the paramedic qualifications if you remember.'

'Yes, you did,' she said flatly, 'and you were the person I most wanted to tell when I'd passed. But the way you acted was like a slap in the face.'

'I know,' he said regretfully, 'but there's a simple answer to that. I hadn't seen you in ages and suddenly you were there, your eyes like stars, delight in every line of you. My need of you just rocked me on my feet. I daren't move or I would have picked you up and carried you off…and there would have been no turning back.'

'So you really do have feelings for me,' she breathed. 'Yet they weren't deep enough for you to act on them without an escape route being available. That isn't what commitment is about, Kane. Having a loophole to scramble through if it doesn't work out.'

He reached across and pulled her around to face him.

'What sort of a man do you think I am, Selina?' he said grittily. 'I don't do things by halves. That's one of the reasons I'm not falling into your lap as fast as you would like.'

That did it.

'How dare you insinuate that I'm out to snare you?' she cried. 'You have some conceit!'

They were brawling like a pair of capricious children, she thought dismally. Had they really come to this?

'Let's go, Kane,' she said in a quieter tone. 'They'll be wondering where I am, and this get-together *is* for me. Also, I rang one of the instructors from the course when I got in to ask him to join us. I was chatting to him today after I'd got my results and he was telling me how lonely he is since moving to the area. It didn't occur to me at the time, but when I thought about it afterwards it seemed a good opportunity for him to meet some new people. So I want to make sure I'm there when he arrives.'

'Yes, of course,' Kane agreed abruptly. Starting the car, he pulled out of the shadows and headed towards the city centre.

She couldn't believe it, Selina thought as high-rise buildings came into view. Kane had told her how much he wanted her...not how much he cared.

And he'd hinted that she was out to 'get him', which brought to mind his comment when he'd told her about the woman who'd caused him so much embarrassment. That *he* preferred to do the 'hunting'.

Well, he could get on with it. Only he needn't expect her to be around waiting to be caught.

When they walked into the wine bar someone shouted, 'Does anyone know where we can find a paramedic?'

The rest of them roared, 'Ye-e-s! There's one here!'

A glass was thrust into her hand and as she was surrounded by their good-natured chaffing, Kane walked towards the bar where Denise was standing.

As Selina watched, the other woman began to walk towards him, hips swaying, the provocative smile on her face and hands outstretched.

She swallowed hard. Denise had been on the fringe of their relationship before, she thought dismally, but now it looked as if she might be wanting to stake a claim. Would Kane allow it?

As she continued to observe them, her face stretched. The russet-haired seductress had walked past him and into the arms of a fair-skinned stranger. As if Kane was aware of her scrutiny, he turned and with a sardonic smile raised his hand in brief salute as if to say, Wrong again!

In the middle of the evening Philip Bassett appeared, and when she saw him hesitating in the doorway Selina went over to him.

'Come and meet my fellow ambulance people,' she said with a welcoming smile, and began to introduce him to those nearest.

Kane was standing with the station officer at the other side of the room and had his back to them as she approached with the elderly training instructor. But when she said, 'Can I introduce Philip Bassett, who until recently was working in health care down south?' he swung round as if she'd put a gun to his back.

'Kane Kavener!' the newcomer exclaimed. 'This is a turn-up for the book! You were the last person I was expecting to see.'

'The feeling is mutual,' Kane said in a voice as tight as a violin string, and Selina thought dismally that here was a face from his past and it wasn't one that he wanted to see.

The moment passed. With a haste she tried to conceal, Selina moved the elderly instructor across to another group of her colleagues and tried to look relaxed.

She would have liked to ask Philip what the connection was between him and Kane but, having seen Kane's expression, she couldn't do it. It would be disloyal to the man she loved. But there was no need to concern herself. Her companion was about to satisfy her curiosity.

'It was a surprise, finding someone I once knew amongst

your people,' he said. 'Kavener and I worked on the same ambulance unit down south. However, there was a nasty scandal and he left. I knew that he'd moved up north after it, but until today didn't know exactly where.'

She had to defend him.

'Kane and I were partners before I went on the training course,' she told him, 'and he's the best.'

He was eyeing her in mild surprise.

'Yes. I'm sure he is. There was never any fault with his performance before. It was just that the man was too attractive for his own good and didn't seem to be aware of it.'

For the rest of the evening she circulated, chatting to everyone but Kane. She was desperate to be alone with him, couldn't bear to see the look on his face, but it would have to wait until he drove her home.

At last it was over and they were on their way back to the village, but now that the opportunity was there she didn't know what to say and it seemed that Kane had no intentions of setting the ball rolling.

Yet she couldn't let him go without getting through to him somehow so when he stopped the car in front of her cottage she reached out and touched his arm.

'Please, Kane, come in for a coffee. I can't leave you looking like that.' Taking the plunge, she went on, 'In fact, I don't want to leave you. We've talked to everyone but each other tonight and I'm miserable. We're playing silly games and we should know better. I'm sorry that I was so horrible and patronising when we were on our way to the wine bar, and if you'll let me I'll show you just how much I regret it.

'You've said that you need me, but you've never said you love me. I don't know, but maybe it's because you've had so little practice when it comes to loving people. If you'll let me, I could help you with that—I've got enough for both of us. I care enough to take you on any terms because I know we're right for each other. So, what do you say?'

She was aware that she hadn't mentioned the fact of he and Philip Bassett knowing each other, and that she should have remarked on it before anything else. But that would have been more likely to drive Kane back to his own place instead of accepting her invitation to enter hers.

He was switching off the engine and getting out of the car, and thankfulness swept over her. She'd got him to herself...for the whole night if he so desired.

As she put the key in the lock he swivelled her round to face him. Speaking for the first time since they'd arrived back, he said, 'I'll come in for the coffee, Selina, but any other delights on offer will have to wait. I would be some prize hypocrite if I made love to you under these circumstances. I don't know what Bassett is going to be telling folk. He was one of those who believed Eve Richards's story and wanted to see me slung out of the service.'

'But it didn't work out like that, did it? You were cleared.'

'Yes, I was cleared. But you know what they say about smoke and mud. One of them is never there without fire, and the other sticks.'

Selina took his hand and pulled him inside, and as they stood with only inches between them in the tiny hallway she said softly, 'He did comment that you are far too attractive for your own good, and I have to agree with that.'

He was unwinding and he laughed low in his throat, 'And what about your charms? I never knew I had so much will-power. When you came breezing into the station today I don't know how I kept my distance.'

'There's no need for that now,' she said softly.

He groaned.

'Don't tempt me. If your guardian angels thought I'd taken advantage of you they might turn into a lynch mob.'

His arms were around her and his mouth only a fraction away as she told him, 'I don't think so. Peter has given up on me, I feel. If he hasn't, he should. Charlie Vaughan I haven't set eyes on since he called round that night, and Gavin has no axe to grind with you. All he and Jill want is to see me happy. So, for goodness' sake, kiss me, Kane.'

He was smiling.

'You're not being fair. Just because I've been bragging about my will-power it doesn't mean that I won't fall by the wayside.'

'I said kiss me, Kane,' she repeated wistfully, and this time he obeyed...to such an extent that her doubts were blotted out, her senses took over and she knew without doubt that if she couldn't have this man, she would want no other.

At last they drew apart. Unbelievably, Kane was gently putting her away from him.

'Nothing has changed, Selina,' he said. 'It would be the easiest thing in the world for me to make love to you, but I'm not going to. Not until all things are even...if that day ever dawns.' And as she stood dazed with disbelief he opened the door and strode out into the night.

When Selina reported for duty after her eight-week absence, it felt strange. For one thing, she wasn't working with Kane any more, which she saw as a mixed blessing, and for another she now had her own vehicle and a trainee to assist her.

During those first few days back on the job Selina heard no comments about him from members of staff and so concluded that Kane's previous acquaintance with Philip

Bassett hadn't been disclosed to anyone but herself by the man in question.

When she'd checked the work rosters on her first morning back she'd seen that they were on the same shifts and hadn't known whether to be glad or sorry.

In truth, she was glad. Because in spite of the frustrated ending to what could have been a night of bliss, she needed to be able to see Kane like she needed to breathe, and if their shifts coincided it was something at least.

She wasn't angry with him. How could she be? After offering herself on a plate, so to speak, he'd still stuck to his principles. But this state of affairs could go on for ever, she thought frequently, and did he once give a thought to how much Josh needed him?

His greeting had been cordial enough when she'd first put in an appearance and as their eyes had met she'd wondered if he ever thought about those moments in the hallway of the cottage.

One thing was for sure, she'd decided glumly. If he did, he wouldn't be telling her. Just in case she got her hopes up.

It was late September and the days were chillier and less bright. The twins had started nursery classes and Josh was in a new class at the village school. All of which made life easier for Jill, to Selina's relief.

The trainee working with her was a nineteen-year-old youth called Elton. He was keen, intelligent and always hungry. He'd been with St John's Ambulance since his early teens, and once he'd been old enough had passed on to trainee status, like many others in the department had done.

Those who'd come from St John's Ambulance were allowed extra points during exams and because of their previous experience had a better chance of passing.

That first morning Selina and Elton were called out to

an elderly lady suffering from dehydration due to excessive vomiting and diarrhoea.

Extreme dehydration could be very serious and she was going to have to be hopsitalised, but first, before leaving her house, they laid her down, loosened her clothing, and gave her sips of water with salt and sugar added.

When she'd had as much as she could take they carried her out to the ambulance and positioned her with her legs raised to allow a better blood supply to vital organs. Then it was off to A and E for further treatment.

Kane and his partner were going out on a call as they arrived back at base. He saluted them briefly as they passed and Selina thought that nothing had changed. They were like ships passing in the night as before.

That feeling became even more pronounced when she discovered that he'd applied to be in charge of one of the fast-response vehicles. He was the ideal person for the job, tough, efficient, used to acting on his own, but the thought of it made him seem even more remote.

She often thought that some quality time together might lead to clearer thinking on both their parts. Not cooped up in an ambulance with Kane, or as a threesome with Josh, delightful though he was.

Selina hungered to be alone with him, just the two of them in a relaxing setting. Unable to hold out any longer, she went to sit beside him one morning in the rest room.

'Hello, stranger,' he said in a low voice. 'To what do I owe this honour?'

'You owe it to me having two tickets for the theatre and not knowing what to do with the extra one,' she told him easily, as if everything was fine between them and she hadn't stage-managed the moment.'

'So in an obscure sort of way, you're asking me to go with you?'

'If you can spare the time.'

'Maybe. When is it?'

'Tonight.'

'Tonight! That's rather short notice.'

'Yes. I know.'

She wasn't going to tell him that she'd bought the tickets on impulse the previous day and, having got the all-clear from Jill and Gavin about minding Josh, had been eager to see how Kane would react to the invitation.

So far so good.

'I suppose I can manage it,' he said. 'It's fortunate that we're working the same hours or you would have had to look elsewhere.'

Selina nodded obediently. Kane knew very well that she wouldn't have done that, but if he wanted to stick with the casual approach, so be it.

'So, which theatre and what time?' he was asking.

'The Adelphi. The show starts at half past seven.'

'I'll call for you just before seven, then?'

She shook her head.

'No. I'll call for you. I asked you out, so I'll do the driving.'

'Just as you like. I take it that we're dressing up?'

'Yes, why not? If spending some time together is to become a yearly event we might as well do it in style.'

Kane was frowning and Selina wished she'd avoided the flippancy. If she didn't watch it the man of iron would change his mind.

As he prepared for the evening ahead Kane found himself singing in the shower, and he didn't have to look far for the reason. The fact that he and Selina would be travelling the road that could lead to heartache once more didn't matter at that moment.

She would be sitting next to him beneath the dim lights of the theatre. He would have her to himself. There would be no call-outs to take her away from him or family commitments, just the two of them in a magical world of their own.

He would concern himself about tomorrow and the days after that as they came along, but tonight would be theirs. A light in the darkness of his self-punishment.

When she stopped her car at the side of the towpath where *The Joshua* was moored he was ready and waiting, resplendent in a light grey suit with dark blue shirt and tie.

He looked stunning, Selina thought as he walked towards the car. Wholesome within and without. Had Kane any idea of his own worth?

As he settled himself into the seat beside her his glance was just as appreciative as hers had been. In a long-sleeved, low-necked, black dress that swirled around her ankles when she was upright, Selina's hair glowed pale gold against the car's dark upholstery.

His senses sprang to life at the sight of her. She was beautiful to him whatever she wore, but tonight she looked incredible. He smiled. If she was out to break down his defences she might just succeed...and where would they go from there?

'So, what's the show?' he asked, bringing his thoughts back to normality as they pulled away from the marina.

She laughed.

'I thought you were never going to ask. It's a musical that's come straight to our city from the London stage.'

'Good. I'm glad it's not *Les Miserables* or *Sweeney Todd* or something similar. They wouldn't fit in with my mood.'

'Why is that?'

'Er...I don't know exactly. Maybe it's because I'm feeling light-hearted for the first time in weeks.'

'And why do you think that is?' she asked innocently.

'It might be because I'm with you.'

'You could be with me all the time if you wanted.'

He shook his head, but he was smiling.

'Please, Selina, not now. Let's just take hold of the opportunity to spend some time together and take it from there.'

'All right,' she agreed meekly, as if that hadn't been the idea all along.

In the close intimacy of the darkened auditorium Kane took Selina's hand in his, and as her fingers lay in the warm comfort of his clasp she told herself that it had been the right idea that they should spend some time on their own.

Tonight they were in tune. She could feel it in his glance, his touch, the way his knee was resting against hers. She should have thought of this before, instead of letting the empty weeks go past.

It was just before the interval that everything changed. She was aware that Kane's attention wasn't on her any more and as she eyed him enquiringly he said, 'Can you smell smoke?'

She sniffed the air around her.

'Er…no. I don't think so.'

He twisted round and eyed the rows of seats behind them.

'I can,' he said uneasily.

'Cigarettes?'

'No. It's a no-smoking building.'

'Look!' she cried. 'You're right. It's coming from the stage!'

Sure enough, within seconds thick black smoke was pouring into the theatre.

As people began to cough and splutter, an announcement came over the loudspeaker system.

'Ladies and gentlemen, we have an emergency. Will you, please, make your way out of the building as quickly as possible? Our staff will direct you.'

Kane was on his feet along with the rest of the audience,

and when she didn't move he said, 'Come on, Selina. This black smoke is lethal and it's moving towards us fast!'

As he spoke the stage curtains burst into flame and the orderly procession making their way to the exits became a stampede, with some people falling in the crush.

Selina was galvanised into action now. After that first moment of amazed disappointment she had gathered her wits and with Kane by her side was holding back the crush while they attended to the fallen.

The onset of the fire was the fastest thing she'd ever seen. One moment they'd been breathing in clean air in safe surroundings and the next they were part of the panic-stricken public fighting their way out of what might soon be an inferno.

The building was cleared without any fatalities, but there were many injured outside, suffering from smoke inhalation, cuts, bruises and more serious things like fractures from being trampled in the desperate rush to safety.

Selina's hair was smoke-blackened, like her face. Kane's light grey suit had taken on a darker shade, but those were minor problems as they helped to treat the injured.

Ambulances were arriving, and as the paramedics scrambled out of them the sight of Kane and Selina kneeling beside those who had come off worst in the panic was greeted with some amazement.

'We need oxygen!' Kane cried. 'Some of these people are asthma sufferers.'

Minutes later, when Selina looked up from bandaging a leg wound on an elderly woman, Kane had gone and a trainee who was hovering told her, 'Kane went with that last ambulance. He wanted to stay with the guy he was treating. He had his chest crushed when he got trampled on inside the theatre.'

She nodded. It was a miracle no one had been killed. The fire service had taken over and the blaze was being brought under control. How it had started no one seemed to know, but an electrical fault was being considered.

At last all the injured had been seen to and the rest of the thwarted theatre-goers had gone. Selina stayed there out on the pavement until there was nothing else she could do and then set off for home, thinking that there was no one more thwarted than she. Every time she and Kane were on the brink of sorting things out, something happened to prevent it.

She was assuming that he was still assisting with the transporting of the injured to the nearest A and E department and when he was likely to surface again she didn't know.

Kane rang at close on midnight.

'So much for our time alone, Selina,' he said ruefully.

'Yes,' she agreed, 'but if the situation had got much worse we might not have lived to regret it. I stayed until everyone had been accounted for and by the time I left they'd put out the fire. How about the casualties?'

'The man who was crushed is in Intensive Care. It was touch and go with him. The rest have either been admitted for observation or sent home. I've only just got in as one of the paramedics developed chest pains and I've been standing in for him.'

'Really? In your smart grey suit?'

'Past tense. It's a trifle soiled at the moment. But I'm keeping you up, aren't I?'

'I wouldn't have gone to bed until I'd heard from you,' she said softly. 'I suppose you got a taxi home.'

'No. Denise gave me a lift. She was in one of the ambulances called out and we met up at A and E.'

'I see.'

'It's happened again, Selina, hasn't it?' he said, ignoring her flat tone. 'We've been sidetracked once again. It's almost as if circumstances are trying to tell us something.'

*   *   *

A call came through for Selina the following morning and she was surprised to hear Sarah's voice on the line. She'd rung a couple of times previously to let her know how little Selina Joy was getting on, but today she had something else to say.

'It's the christening at eleven o'clock next Sunday,' she said. 'Will you and Kane be available to be godparents? I know it's short notice, but it's the only Sunday my husband can get off work. He's with the police.'

'I'm free this weekend,' Selina told her, 'and Kane isn't working either, but I don't know if he's made other plans. If you'll hang on, I'll go and ask him.'

He'd just got back from an emergency and was having a drink and a quick bite when she went up to him.

'Sarah is on the phone, asking if we can be godparents to Selina Joy this Sunday,' she said with a tentative smile. 'Are you free?'

He nodded.

'Yes. What time?'

'Eleven o'clock.'

'OK. No problem.'

'Right. I'll tell her that we're both available, then.' And off she went with the feeling that Kane was being a bit optimistic if he thought them being together at the baby's christening presented no problem with their track record.

But, she thought with the beginnings of anticipation, this time it had to be right. There would only be a problem if they created one and *she* wouldn't be doing that.

She'd never forgotten helping to bring Sarah's baby into the world. It had been her first maternity emergency and after her initial trepidation it had been a wonderful thing to be part of.

'I'll pick you up on Sunday if you like,' Kane said when

she came off the phone, and as she eyed him warily he added, 'I promise to be on my best behaviour.'

'That's just the trouble,' she said. 'I'm fed up with you being on your best behaviour. You never get the chance to be anything else. And as to the offer, I suppose it's sensible that we only use the one car.'

As if she hadn't spoken, he said calmly, 'Where is this christening to take place?'

'A small Methodist church not far from here, and afterwards we're invited back to the house.'

He pursed his lips.

'I'm not sure about the last bit.'

'We don't need to stay long. It would be churlish to refuse.'

'Yes, I suppose so,' he agreed, and then to her surprise said, 'Aren't we as godparents supposed to commemorate the occasion with a gift of some sort?'

'Correct. How about a silver bracelet that will extend as she gets bigger?'

'Yes. Why not? Would there be time to have it engraved?'

'I suppose so if we get a move on.'

'Right. You get the bracelet and I'll have it engraved. Agreed?'

'What with?'

'I don't know. I'll think of something appropriate.'

When she asked Josh if he wanted to go to the christening with her, he said, 'No. Uncle Gavin and Aunty Jill will let me stay there until you come back.'

'No doubt they will, but are you sure?' she asked.

'Yes,' he said firmly.

And so it was just the two of them who presented themselves at the church at a quarter to eleven on Sunday morning.

Selina had chosen to wear a pale green wool suit with cream hat and shoes and when Kane had called for her he said just the one word. 'Smart!'

But his glance said a lot more than that and she had to remind herself that if it hadn't been for the invitation to the christening it would have been just one more weekend without him.

'Have you got the bracelet?' she asked.

'Yes.'

He reached into his pocket and took out a flat square box that had been gift-wrapped for the occasion.

'I'd like to have seen the engraving,' she protested mildly.

'You'll see it when they unwrap it,' he said blandly, and she had to be content with that.

All the members of both families were there, and the two paramedics were welcomed with open arms to the special event. No one seemed to find it odd that they'd been asked to be godparents, and during the simple ceremony the minister referred to their part in the birth of Selina Joy.

Kane's expression was giving nothing away and Selina wondered what he was thinking. She knew he loved children. The way he treated Josh was proof of that. But how was he going to ever have any of his own if he stayed so aloof from the kind of relationships that resulted in family life?

Or was it just with her he was so wary? Because of her background and his assumption that she was vulnerable?

'What were you so deep in thought about during the service?' he asked as they drove to the small terraced house where Sarah and her husband lived.

'I was thinking how good you look in a suit,' she fibbed.

'Oh, yeah?'

'Mmm.'

'Now tell me what you were really thinking.'

'I was thinking what a good father you would make.'

He groaned. 'Don't, Selina. I promised to be on my best behaviour and I'm expecting you to be on yours.'

'The bracelet is lovely,' Sarah said when they joined the rest of the party. 'We've just opened it, and am I right in thinking that the inscription inside was your idea, Kane?'

He shrugged.

Stepping forward, Selina said, 'Let me see.'

It read, 'To Selina Joy on her baptism. May she grow in grace and beauty as her namesake.'

She felt her colour rise. Kane could do something like this, tender and loving, that would make anyone reading it think they had a special relationship—yet all the while they were going nowhere.

When they were getting ready to leave, after sharing a buffet meal with the two families, Sarah's husband got to his feet and proposed a toast.

'To the ambulance service, and to Selina and Kane.' When everyone solemnly raised their glasses, she thought that having their names coupled together looked like being the nearest they were going to get.

'The christening was lovely, wasn't it?' she said dreamily as they drove home.

'Yes, it was,' Kane said briefly, and she felt that he was waiting for her to say something else, maybe about the bracelet. But she wasn't going to oblige. In future any meaningful remarks had to come from him, and when they reached the cottage she showed no signs of lingering.

He reached out and took hold of her arm.

'What's the rush? Are you upset about the bracelet? That I didn't consult you first?'

'No. What you'd had engraved inside was very nice,' she said awkwardly.

'Nice? Is that it?'

She sighed.

'What do you want me to say? I feel as if every now and then you throw me a crumb and it's supposed to suffice until the next time you notice I'm there.'

'Notice you!' he cried. 'I see you all the time, even when you're not there. Don't make a mockery of my feelings for you.'

'*Me* make a mockery of your feelings for me! You're managing to do that all by yourself.' Easing her arm out of his grasp, she opened the car door and went inside the cottage, half hoping that he might follow. But no sooner had she closed the door than she heard him drive off.

CHAPTER TEN

IT WAS Josh's birthday a fortnight later, and as it conveniently fell on Selina's day off she was taking him, the twins and three of his school friends to the cinema in the afternoon and then having them all back for tea.

Embroiled in preparations the night before, she was interrupted by a ring on the doorbell. When she answered it Kane was standing there.

'Kane,' she breathed, taken aback at the sight of him. 'To what do we owe the honour?'

'I've brought a present for Josh.'

Stepping back to let him over the threshold, she said in surprise, 'I wasn't aware that you knew it was his birthday.'

'Really? He told me ages ago.'

She found herself laughing.

'I hope he didn't also tell you what he would like you to buy him.'

'Er...no. I worked it out for myself. I hope he hasn't got a scooter.'

'No, he hasn't, although it has been mentioned several times that he would like one.'

He smiled.

'All the youngsters have got them at the moment and he *will* be ten tomorrow. He's a sensible lad. I don't think you need worry.'

There was a warm feeling inside her. Whatever might be lacking in their relationship, Kane hadn't forgotten Josh. When he woke in the morning the scooter would put everything else in the shade.

She wanted to throw her arms around Kane and tell him

how much it would mean to Josh that he'd remembered. Instead, she said stiltedly, 'It's good of you to think of him, Kane. These are the times when he misses his dad.'

He met her eyes levelly.

'You surely don't think I would forget him, do you, Selina? I keep away because I don't want to cause him any hurt, the same as I try to keep a clear head where you're concerned.'

There were many things she could have said to that but she felt as if they'd already been said. She could only put her point of view forward so many times.

'Is Josh asleep?' he asked, and she sensed that he'd read her mind and didn't want a discourse about anything other than Josh's birthday.

'Yes. He was when I last looked.'

'Good. I'll go and get the scooter out of the car and then I'm shooting off. I have an appointment.'

'Oh.'

She would have liked to have asked who with, but maybe it was best if she didn't know. What she didn't know about she wouldn't fret about.

'Is he having a party?' Kane asked when he'd deposited the gift-wrapped parcel which, by its shape, was easily identifiable.

'Sort of. I'm taking six of them to the cinema in the afternoon and then they're coming back here for tea.'

'Do you need a hand? Remember, we do have the same days off.'

She found herself smiling with pleasure.

'That would be lovely. I need as many hands as I can get, plus eyes in the back of my head and built-in radar.'

'So Jill isn't going with you?'

'No. I've insisted that she has an afternoon to herself.'

'What time are you setting off?' he asked.

'Half past one, and we're using the children's favourite mode of transport.'

'What's that?'

'The top of the bus. Young ones who go everywhere by car are thrilled when they get the chance to travel by bus.'

He laughed.

'When we were kids it was the other way round.'

Selina was feeling all warm inside. This was hardly a romantic tryst, but there was peace between them and a precious sort of friendliness.

Yet they'd been friends from the start, hadn't they? Apart from the odd fraying of tempers. Kane's scruples were preventing any deeper commitment on his part. Could she settle for just being friends? She didn't think so.

He was ready to go.

'I'll see you tomorrow, then.'

'Yes,' she said brightly.

When Josh came downstairs the next morning the first thing he saw was the strange-looking parcel that contained the scooter. Selina had bought him a PlayStation and his grand-dad had sent money to buy him the strip of his favourite football team, but it was Kane's gift he zoomed in on first.

'It's from Kane,' she said, having no doubts about what his reaction would be.

'Cool!' he whooped. 'So he does still like us after all.'

Her smile was tender.

'I think we might even say that he loves us, but he has things on his mind that stop him from saying so.'

Josh was only half listening. He was opening the back door and heading for the flagged path that led to the bottom of the garden, and as he whizzed along it Selina thought that the scooter wasn't the only surprise of the day. He had yet to discover that Kane was going to the cinema with them and coming back afterwards.

'Cool!' he cried again when she told him. 'What a super birthday!'

They were the only ones on the top of the city-bound bus and every time tree branches banged noisily against the windows the children watched goggle-eyed, much to the amusement of the two adults.

They were seated together behind their young charges and Selina was experiencing the same feeling she'd had on the day they'd gone to Blackpool, that they were on a family outing, mother, father and children...and that Dave would approve.

She snuggled down in her seat, happy with her thoughts, and when Kane turned and caught her expression he said, 'So what is it that's making you look so satisfied with life?'

'Having you beside me,' she said with grateful candour. 'I feel as if *I'm* having a birthday too.'

He lifted her hand off her lap and, taking it in his big capable fist, squeezed it gently.

'You are the most contented person I've ever met, Selina. It doesn't take a lot to make you happy, does it?'

'Not normally,' she teased gently, 'but of late I've been discovering that in some areas it's a very hard-won commodity.'

'That being a dig at me, of course.'

'Mmm.'

'So why don't we pretend for today that my reputation is as white as driven snow and that I'm not the complicated person that I usually am?'

He was smiling, but she sensed there was seriousness behind it, and when he went on to say, 'I can't be disciplining myself all the time, can I?' she knew she was right.

'No, indeed,' she told him. 'As far as I'm concerned, there's nothing to discipline yourself for.'

'We've already been down that road a few times,' he protested mildly. 'Let's take a side turning for now, eh?'

'I couldn't agree more,' she replied.

The bus pulled into the terminus at that moment. They saw their small charges safely off and proceeded to where one of the cinemas was showing a children's film.

Selina had been acutely conscious of Kane's nearness on the bus—his thigh touching hers, dark eyes watching her every movement, the mouth that told her the things that his voice wouldn't put into words.

In the darkened cinema it was worse, and it awakened memories of their disastrous visit to the theatre. But this time they weren't alone. They had three children on either side of them, yet it didn't make her longing any less.

But there was ice cream to be bought, popcorn, sweets and a visit to the toilets for the twins, while all the time she wanted to stay there at Kane's side, revelling in his nearness.

And if there hadn't been all that to deal with, there was Josh next to Kane, full of excited chatter. But it was his day, wasn't it? With the scooter waiting for him back at home and the man who he already saw as a father figure sitting beside him, he was a happy child.

They went back to the house afterwards and had crisps, tiny sandwiches, sausages on sticks, yoghurts, ice cream and the rest.

And now the small guests had gone home, clutching balloons and goody bags.

'Whew!' Selina said. 'I'm going to put the kettle on.'

Kane had just come in from the garden where he'd been watching Josh on the scooter, and when she saw his expression she said, 'What is it?'

'Your son,' he said heavily.

'What about him?'

'Josh has just asked me why, if I love you both, I don't become his new dad.'

'I see,' she said slowly, as their discussion earlier in the day came back to mind.

'I wouldn't have thought you would use Josh to manipulate me,' he went on, 'but you must have said something to put the idea in his head, and if there's one person that I don't want to upset, it's him.'

She was observing him with hurt and rising anger.

'Me use Josh to manipulate you! How dare you? What kind of a person do you think I am? It's true, we did have a conversation about you this morning. When he saw the scooter he said that you must still like us after all, and I...I said that I thought that you might even love us, but that you weren't ready to do anything about it. How was I to know that he would try to give you a push in the right direction? Though heaven only knows, you need one!'

The moment the words had left Selina's mouth she was appalled. Here was a man of honour who was ignoring his own desires out of consideration for herself, and she'd just berated him as if he were some sort of weakling.

Kane's expression told her that he'd got the message. Well and truly! Here we go again, she thought. Back to square one.

'I thought you understood why I've been holding back, but obviously I was wrong,' he said, tight-lipped. 'Why do I keep forgetting that they who travel alone have only themselves to please? I'm going to say goodbye to Josh and then I'm going, and in future, if you have anything to say to me, don't use your son as the go-between.'

As Kane drove back to the boat Selina wasn't the only one who was wishing she'd chosen her words more carefully.

Josh had taken him completely unawares with his guileless question, and because he'd been in a state of longing and regret all day he'd let it get to him to such an extent that he'd taken it out on Selina.

It hadn't been fair, but it had shown him one thing. She thought he was the kind of man who hadn't the guts to make a proper commitment to a woman, and the hurt had gone deep.

With regard to Josh, it had made him see even more clearly that he couldn't keep blowing hot and cold with the child. One moment in his life and the next out of it.

He wasn't doing either of them any favours. It was time to move on…again. Just when he'd thought his wanderings were over.

'It's the best birthday I've ever had,' Josh said blissfully as the day came to a close.

'Good,' she said. 'I'm glad you've enjoyed it.'

'I've sorted things out with Kane,' he said suddenly.

'Really? In what way?'

He was observing her cautiously.

'I've told him that I want him to be my new dad.'

'And what did he say to that?'

As if she didn't know!

'He promised to think about it.'

And immediately jumped to the wrong conclusions, she thought miserably, causing her to retaliate angrily, which had made matters worse. Much worse!

It was the word 'manipulate' that had made her see red. It made her sound conniving and cunning, and almost made her wish herself back to the state of muted misery she'd been in before they'd met.

If that was how he saw her, a rethink was needed. But maybe she should have done that long ago, when the first tender shoots of their relationship had been springing up.

For the rest of the weekend Selina was miserable and on edge. But that was nothing to how she felt when, on reporting for duty on Monday night, she was told that Kane had handed in his notice.

It was Elton who told her.

'Guess what, Selina?' he said. 'Kane's leaving. He's been in to see the boss and he's going at the end of the month.'

She felt the colour drain from her face. That was going too far. How could he hurt her like this? She needed him and so did Josh, but it looked as if he didn't need them.

When they came face to face in the rest room he looked her in the eye and said evenly, 'Hello, Selina. How are you?'

'How do you think I am?' she said in an angry whisper. 'I can't believe what you're doing. What are you hoping to achieve?'

'Peace of mind, maybe.'

'Peace of mind, my foot,' she snapped. 'I would never have had you down as a quitter. Well, the best of luck wherever you go. I would suggest a monastery. You've changed your job twice because of women, so maybe you'd have more luck in an all-male establishment.'

Her voice trailed away. He looked tired. There was a sort of weary resignation about him that was nothing like his usual cool competence. What was the use of ranting on about what he'd done? If Kane wanted to go it must be because he no longer had any use for Josh and herself.

'I'm sorry,' she muttered. 'Don't take any notice of me…not that you ever do.'

He'd been silent all through her tirade, which was upsetting her even more, but now he did have one thing to say and it wasn't going to make her feel any better.

'I'll leave it to you to tell Josh what's happening. If you don't mind.'

'Oh, yes, of course. That will be really easy. Telling him that you're off to pastures new.'

If he'd anything to say to that she wasn't going to listen to it. He'd just had an emergency passed on to him from an amusement arcade in the city centre, and as the big metal doors rolled noisily upwards Kane and his young assistant drove out to meet the perils of the night.

No one seemed to know where Kane was moving to, and to anyone who asked he was extremely noncommittal, due to the fact that he didn't know himself. Though it seemed logical that he should stay in healthcare, but in some other town or city.

He would be with the unit until the end of the month, which left him with just over three weeks to do. Selina had wondered a few times what he was going to do about the boat. Would he sell it? Sail off into the sunset...or what?

Whatever he did, she wasn't going to be part of it and that was the hardest thing to bear. But, she told herself glumly, she'd been coping before Kane had come into her life and she would continue to do so.

Thankfully, Josh was absorbed in his own little world. He had no idea that his innocent question had triggered the present situation, and as she watched over him lovingly Selina was happy for it to stay that way.

There was just one week to go before Kane went out of their lives and Selina was having to admit that it was no good trying to be positive and forward-looking when there was nothing to look forward to.

They'd spoken only briefly in the past two weeks and then it had been about the job. Selina had decided that if there was any mention of farewell gatherings, she wasn't going to join in. It was all painful enough, without self-inflicted punishment.

On a dark October evening she was surprised to find Philip Bassett on her doorstep, and in response to her surprised expression he said, 'I hope I'm not intruding, Selina.'

'Of course not,' she said as she stepped back to let him in. 'I said that you were welcome to call any time. What can I do for you, Philip. Anything special?'

He cleared his throat. 'It's what I can do for Kane that I've come about.'

Her eyes widened but she didn't interrupt.

'I've heard that he's leaving and I'm concerned that it might have something to do with me appearing on the scene. You might wonder why I'm telling *you* this instead of him, but from the way you defended him that night when I joined you at the wine bar, I sense that you're a good friend of his.'

'I might be if he would give me the chance,' she said flatly. 'But what happened before he came here has scarred him. For reasons that I won't go into he's a very private person with deep moral convictions, and even though it was all proved to be lies, that and a couple of other things that have happened while he's been here have made matters worse. And I have to admit that your appearance didn't improve things.'

Philip sighed.

'That's what I thought, and I have to tell you that I carry a burden of guilt concerning that unpleasant episode with Eve Richards. No one knew it at the time but the woman was mentally ill. She'd done it before, making those sorts of accusations. But she was so convincing as she played the victim that we all believed her. Myself most of all. I'm a prudish sort of person and I was all for Kane being slung out of the service.

'Fortunately everyone wasn't as biased as I was and when Eve was investigated it all came out and Kane was cleared. As you may already know, he'd decided to move elsewhere to get away from her advances and once the inquiry was over he carried on with his plans and moved to this area.'

'And is now about to move again,' she said sombrely, 'because he still feels tainted by what happened and is letting it come between us.'

'So you care for him?'

'Yes, I do.'

'Then somebody needs to talk some sense to him. Make him change his mind. The man is crazy to think of turning his back on someone like you.'

'You're right,' she said, fired with new determination. 'Kane has a boat on the canal near here. I'll go to him and make him see sense.'

Philip nodded.

'Good. Kane deserves better than he's had. And I for one will sleep easier in my bed if I know that his world has righted itself.'

When he'd gone Selina phoned Jill and asked her to come over so that Josh wasn't alone while she went on what was now an urgent errand. As she waited, Selina thought that Philip's visit had been just what she needed. She'd been too compliant, too willing to understand, instead of making Kane see that living in the past wasn't going to get either of them anywhere. She wasn't going to leave until she'd convinced him.

'Oh, no!' she cried as the marina came in sight. *The Joshua* was in darkness on the still waters of the canal.

'Kane, where are you?' she muttered in the silent night. 'Not here, obviously.'

The impetus that had given wings to her feet had gone. She couldn't stay and wait for him. It might be hours before he showed up. What she had to say to him would have to wait until tomorrow.

'You're soon back,' Jill said a few minutes later. 'Wouldn't he listen?'

'Kane wasn't there,' she said fretfully. 'I should have anticipated that might be the case.'

'Don't give up, Selina,' her sister-in-law said. 'There's always tomorrow.'

'Yes, I know. But enough time has been wasted already,' she wailed.

She wasn't to know it, but Kane had only been a short distance away. He'd gone to take a last look at Lock-Keeper's Cottage and had returned only minutes after her visit.

He'd stood pensively outside the only house that he'd ever really wanted to live in, and the doubts that were crowding his mind had seemed to multiply.

Why was he so determined on self-punishment when he'd done no wrong? he asked himself. Because he was too stubborn for his own good? Because a child's innocent remark had shown him what he ought to do? Why was he hurting the two people who would make life worth living if he would only let them? He wished he knew.

But Selina wasn't just anybody. She was beautiful, kind...and vulnerable, and he still wasn't convinced that he was the right one for her.

It was only a matter of days before his notice was up and he was no nearer to clarifying his thoughts. Where was the quick decisiveness that had always carried him through before?

Selina barely slept. The words she was going to say to Kane kept going through her mind, and she couldn't wait for morning to come.

But the moment she set foot in the ambulance station she and Elton were given the first emergency of the shift and Kane and his companion the second.

'Hi!' he said when they met briefly while the calls were coming through.

'Hello, yourself,' she replied, and controlled the urge to tell him that she was desperate to talk to him. Caution told her that if he had advance warning Kane would have time to strengthen his arguments, and she didn't want that.

She intended to sweep away all his reasons for leaving. Make him see once and for all that they were meant to be together and that there was no way she was going to be sidetracked.

But it wasn't something she could achieve in five minutes and so she exchanged brief greetings with him and went on her way.

The emergency she'd been directed to was of the direst kind. A couple of youngsters, brother and sister, had been paddling across the shallowest part of a fast-flowing river. The boy had crossed without incident, but the girl had been swept off her feet by the force of the current and had gone over a nearby weir.

That would have been serious enough, but as she'd gone over she'd caught her foot in debris and was hanging down head first, with the water washing over her face every few seconds.

The boy's cries had attracted the attention of a man fishing lower down the river and when he'd seen the girl's plight he'd held out his landing net for her to hold onto so that she could keep her head above water.

But that had been all he'd been able to do, short of throwing himself into the dangerous current to try and free her, so he'd told the boy to ring emergency services on his mobile.

Selina was the first to arrive and as she and Elton flung themselves out of the ambulance the boy on the bank cried, 'It's Lucy! My sister ! She's got her leg stuck. She's going to drown!'

Not if I can help it, Selina thought grimly as she ripped off her jacket and kicked off her shoes.

'Stay here and wait for the police and firefighters,' she told Elton. 'And look after the boy. He's wet through. Wrap him in a blanket.'

Poised above the grey swirling waters, she said, 'I'm going in. That child has taken in too much water already. I've got to get her free. Keep shouting to her, Elton. She's only just conscious.'

The moment she entered the water Selina felt the force of the current, yet she managed to get across to the girl. But just as she came within reach, her own feet were swept from under her and she found herself being taken down-river.

When an overhanging branch appeared she grabbed it and hung on grimly, feeling as if her arms were being wrenched out of their sockets. Then she was swimming back up the river. But it was no use. The same thing happened again and again, and the fear of losing the child was filling her with sick desperation.

The fourth time she managed to hang onto a piece of rock jutting out of the weir and got a hold on the girl's arm. As she looked down Selina saw that the child's foot was caught in a piece of tangled scrap metal amongst debris that had piled up with the force of the water.

She was exhausted now from battling the current, and very cold, but there was no way she was going to let go of the child. Yet how was she going to get her free without loosening her hold on her arm?

'I'm here, Lucy!' she cried above the noise of the water. 'Help will be here soon. Hold on, little one.'

But there was no answer from the child and Selina thought that if *she* was cold, how much more so was small Lucy?

Up to then there'd been no time to take note of what

was happening on the bank, but now she could hear the screech of sirens on the raw morning air and she prayed that they would be in time.

As two wet male heads bobbed up beside her in the fast-flowing waters it seemed that her prayers had been answered, and when she heard Kane's voice crying for her to hold on she listened in amazed disbelief.

The other man was in policeman's uniform and as she watched he was swept downriver just as she had been.

'Keep talking to her!' Kane bellowed as he came up beside them. 'The poor little lass is hardly with us any more. I'm going to see if I can release her foot.'

It must have been only seconds but it seemed like a lifetime before he said, 'She's free, Selina. Strike out for the bank. I'll support her on the other side.'

At that moment they were rejoined by the policeman, who'd done the same as she had and swum back, and a burly fireman who'd jumped in to join them. Suddenly what had seemed like an impossible task became easy as four strong swimmers brought the girl to safety.

When they were on dry land once more Selina dragged herself onto the grass and lay there, gasping, while Kane began to resuscitate the limp figure of the girl.

At last she began to retch and water spurted from her mouth, raising a cheer from the anxious watchers. Her ankle was cut and badly bruised where it had been caught, but there didn't appear to be any fracture. She lay there, pale and puffy-faced and shivering uncontrollably. Kane said to his trainee and an anxious Elton, 'Get this young lady on board my ambulance fast. Strip her wet clothes off and wrap her in a blanket. While you're doing that I want a quick word with Selina.'

She was sitting up now. Wet, bedraggled and blue with cold. Her hands were bleeding from the stones and branches that she'd been thrown up against, and Kane wanted to hold her close and never let her go. But it wasn't the moment to be pandering to his own needs.

The girl had to be his priority, but he couldn't have left the scene without making sure that Selina was all right. She'd risked her life for Lucy and would have given no thought to her own danger. But what would he and Josh have done without her?

'How's Lucy?' she croaked.

'Coming round...thank goodness. But, like you, she's very cold and her temperature isn't reassuring. We're taking you both to A and E to be treated for hypothermia and whatever other injuries you might have. And, Selina, my dearest love,' he went on, his voice roughening, 'don't ever frighten me like that again.'

'I didn't do it on purpose,' she whispered through chattering teeth.

He touched her wet cheek gently and a smile tugged at his mouth.

'Oh, I don't know. It's surprising what some women will do to get my attention.'

'I don't understand how you came to be here,' she said weakly.

'That explanation can come later. I've got to get little Lucy to Casualty. Elton will take you, and as soon as you're in the ambulance get your wet clothes off and wrap yourself in a blanket.'

'What about *your* wet things?'

He shrugged. 'As soon as I've got Lucy sorted. I wasn't in the water as long as you.'

He squeezed her hand gently and ran back to where his ambulance was waiting.

The fact that she was an adult and her extreme exertions had kept her blood flowing with some degree of warmth while in the swollen river had saved Selina from any extensive hypothermia, but the doctor on duty in A and E had insisted that she stay in hospital overnight.

Lucy was a different matter. The long immersion in the water with such restricted movement had left her in a dangerous condition and she'd been taken to Intensive Care where her body warmth was being raised slowly and carefully to avoid shock.

When Selina had arrived, with Elton hovering over her protectively, Kane had been in with the trauma team who'd been waiting for Lucy, giving his report of temperature readings and details of how long she'd been in the water and how long it had taken her to respond to resuscitation.

But once that had been done he'd gone to find Selina, and as he'd drawn back the curtains of the cubicle where she'd been placed until a bed became free, all the things that had been bugging him for so long had settled into place.

He'd got his priorities right at last. Taken the blinkers off. He'd realised now that it didn't matter a damn what others thought of him. That had been his stupid pride blocking his vision. It was what Selina thought about him that mattered, and right from the start she'd believed in him.

It had taken the thought of losing her for ever to make him see sense, yet after the way he'd behaved he didn't deserve her. Would she give him another chance? he'd wondered as he'd monitored Lucy on the way to hospital.

And now here she was, with her brightness dimmed, mud in her hair, her face pale, and as always, when he appeared, with questions in her eyes.

But today he had some answers. He hoped they would be the ones she wanted to hear.

'How are you?' he asked as he took her hand and perched on the side of the bed.

'All right, I suppose,' she said quietly. 'But now I've had time to think I'm overcome with horror at the thought that I could have left Josh without mother or father. Yet I had to do it, Kane.'

'Of course you did, Selina. That's what our job is all about. And regarding Josh, if the unthinkable had happened, I would have taken care of him.'

'How could you have done that when you're going away?' she asked tearfully.

'I'm not going anywhere,' he said gently. 'It took the thought of losing you to make me see sense. When the message came through from young Elton that you were in trouble, we were only a couple of miles away and I couldn't get to you quickly enough.

'However, it was long enough for me to take a good look at myself, and I wasn't happy with what I saw. I've been so wrapped up in my own reservations that I couldn't see straight. But I can now.'

He lifted a strand of her matted hair and let it slide slowly through his fingers.

'Will you marry me, Selina?'

'Oh, yes!' she said fervently. 'I thought you'd never ask. I was going to give you some straight talking the moment I got the chance. I just couldn't let you leave without putting up a fight. But that awful episode down by the river seems to have done it for me.'

She was smiling now. Selina at her most radiant.

'Philip Bassett came to see me last night,' she told him, 'and he feels very guilty about his behaviour when you had that awful experience at the other place. He certainly won't be saying anything derogatory about you to anyone.'

He smiled back.

'I don't care if he does. The only people who matter are you and Josh, and what do you think he'll have to say when he hears our news?'

'Cool!' she told him laughingly. 'And you can't get

higher approval than that. He will know then that you do love us and that you do want to be his new dad.'

'I can't think of anything I want more,' he said tenderly, 'and I have to say that, given the choice, I would have preferred my future wife not to be blanket-wrapped when I kissed her. But we'll make up for that another time, won't we, Selina?'

'We will indeed,' she breathed, and as he took her in his arms the day that had started with doubts and uncertainty became safe and secure, and she knew that was how it would always be with Kane by her side.

'I'm going to have to go,' he said at last. 'Elton and the other lad will have explained what happened to the station officer, but with you in here and myself absent they'll be two vehicles short. And I have to go and cancel my notice if they'll let me. It shouldn't be a problem as I've been asked to change my mind a few times.

'I'll get back as soon as I can and in the meantime I'll let Jill know what's happened so she can bring Josh to see you.'

She nodded.

'Yes, and maybe by then I'll have had a bath, washed my hair and been provided with something to wear. Hopefully not a flannelette nightdress.'

When Josh appeared, holding tightly to Jill's hand, Selina held out her arms and he rushed into them. Her eyes met her sister-in-law's above his blond head and Jill said quietly, 'He thought he was going to lose you, too.'

Selina nodded and held him even closer.

'I'm all right, sweetheart,' she told him. 'The doctor is only keeping me in for a while because I got very cold in the water. You'll be all right staying with Aunty Jill and Uncle Gavin for the night, won't you?'

He nodded, still without speaking, and Jill said gently, 'I'll leave you two on your own and come back later.'

'I've got something to ask you, Josh,' Selina said when she'd gone.

'What?' he asked in a muffled voice with his face still pressed up against her.

'Supposing a fairy came and said she would grant you one wish. What would you ask for?'

'That I could take a packed lunch instead of having school dinners.'

She smiled.

'You can think of something more exciting than that, surely. Something that you want most in all the world.'

He lifted his head slowly.

'You mean like Kane coming to live with us and being my dad?'

'Yes. That's what I mean,' she said softly.

'And is he?'

'Yes,' Kane said from the doorway of the ward. 'He is.'

'Cool!' Josh cried, and wondered why they were laughing.

Selina was home, none the worse for her ordeal. To the relief of everyone concerned, Lucy was progressing satisfactorily and would soon be back with her family.

Her parents had been to see Selina before she'd been discharged from the hospital to express their grateful thanks and she'd known just how she would have felt in their place.

To lose a partner was awful, but there was nothing to equal the agony of losing a child.

And now, on a crisp Saturday morning, Kane was insisting that the three of them go for a stroll along the canal bank.

The wedding preparations were under way and as it was

in just a fortnight's time Selina had protested mildly that she had shopping to do. But such was her joy in knowing that he loved her that she would have jumped into the same canal if he'd asked her to. Though it wasn't likely as she'd only just got over a previous wetting.

As they drew near Lock-Keeper's Cottage she said in surprise, 'Look, Josh! Our favourite house has been sold. What a shame. I always dreamt of living there.'

'Me, too,' Kane said casually. Taking her hand in his, he put a key on her outstretched palm.

'What's that for?' she asked curiously.

'It's to open the door of what is going to be our house...if you want it. I've made an offer, but I'm only prepared to go ahead if it's what you want.'

'What I want!' she breathed. 'Of course it's what I want. But can we afford it?'

'Yes, if I sell the boat.'

Josh was looking down at the ground and so far he hadn't said anything, but they both knew what he was thinking. The boat had his name on it. It was his favourite place.

'Aren't we forgetting something?' she said. '*I* have a house to sell.'

Kane shook his head.

'I want to be responsible for providing my new family with a home. I don't want it to rely on the sale of your house.'

'There's that pride of yours again,' she said tenderly. 'We're going to be partners, Kane. *Equal* partners. Sharing and caring. I know how much you both love the boat. Let it be my gift to you.'

Josh was looking at them with hopeful eyes and Kane smiled.

'All right, partner, if that's what you want.' He drew her

into his arms. 'It becomes a magical word when *you* say it.'

'What does?'

'Partners.'

Modern Romance™
...seduction and
passion guaranteed

Tender Romance™
...love affairs that
last a lifetime

Sensual Romance™
...sassy, sexy and
seductive

Blaze
...sultry days and
steamy nights

Medical Romance™
...medical drama on
the pulse

Historical Romance™
...rich, vivid and
passionate

27 new titles every month.

*With all kinds of Romance for
every kind of mood...*

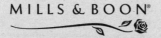

MILLS & BOON®

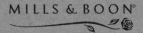

MILLS & BOON®

Medical Romance™

MORE THAN CARING *by Josie Metcalfe*

Lauren Scott has never found it easy to invest in relationships – instead she's invested her care in nursing her patients. Then handsome hospital administrator Marc Fletcher comes to her rescue and it seems Lauren has finally found a man she can trust. But Marc has also been running away from relationships and, if they are to have a chance together, Lauren must persuade Marc to accept some TLC in return.

HER UNEXPECTED FAMILY *by Gill Sanderson*

When Nurse Tessa Calvert helped a troubled woman on her radio show it turned out to be the rebellious young daughter of her new boss, A&E consultant James Armstrong – and he was furious at Tessa's inappropriate advice! Despite their explosive beginning, both James and Tessa soon felt the powerful attraction emerging between them…

THE VISITING SURGEON *by Lucy Clark*

Surgeon Susie Monahan has no intention of acting on the instant attraction between herself and gorgeous visiting orthopaedic professor Jackson Myers. She's been badly hurt before – and he's only in Brisbane for a week. Despite her fears, she finds herself longing to hold him in her arms and never let him go!

On sale 4th October 2002

Available at most branches of WH Smith, Tesco, Martins, Borders, Eason, Sainsbury's and all good paperback bookshops.

0902/03a

Don't miss *Book Two* of this BRAND-NEW 12 book collection 'Bachelor Auction'.

Who says money can't buy love?

On sale 4th October

FREE
2 BOOKS
AND A SURPRISE GIFT!

We would like to take this opportunity to thank you for reading this Mills & Boon® book by offering you the chance to take TWO more specially selected titles from the Medical Romance™ series absolutely FREE! We're also making this offer to introduce you to the benefits of the Reader Service™ —

- ★ FREE home delivery
- ★ FREE monthly Newsletter
- ★ FREE gifts and competitions
- ★ Exclusive Reader Service discount
- ★ Books available before they're in the shops

Accepting these FREE books and gift places you under no obligation to buy; you may cancel at any time, even after receiving your free shipment. Simply complete your details below and return the entire page to the address below. *You don't even need a stamp!*

YES! Please send me 2 free Medical Romance books and a surprise gift. I understand that unless you hear from me, I will receive 4 superb new titles every month for just £2.55 each, postage and packing free. I am under no obligation to purchase any books and may cancel my subscription at any time. The free books and gift will be mine to keep in any case.

M2ZEC

Ms/Mrs/Miss/Mr ....Initials ....
BLOCK CAPITALS PLEASE

Surname ....

Address ....

....

....Postcode ....

Send this whole page to:
UK: FREEPOST CN81, Croydon, CR9 3WZ
EIRE: PO Box 4546, Kilcock, County Kildare (stamp required)